THE GREEN HELIX

THE GREEN HELIX

E. C. TUBB

WILDSIDE PRESS

CHAPTER 1

THE MISSING SHIPS

THE sound was a thin, high-pitched keening; a grating whine, hovering on the very edge of audibility. It sang from the metal of the deck plates and bulkheads, whispered from the layers of thick insulation, quivered from the very air. It was a nerve-racking sound; vibrating through flesh and bone and sinew, sending little trickles of irritation running over tender skin and jarring at unstable emotions. Yet it was a good sound, for while they heard it they were safe.

Caleb leaned back in the cushioned softness of the pilot's chair and grinned at Wilner. "It won't be long now," he said reassuringly. "This hop is almost over."

"Good!" The astrogator shifted nervously in his seat and ran a hand through his thin red hair. A thick scattering of freckles stood clearly against the stark whiteness of his skin, and high on one cheek a muscle twitched in a nervous spasm.

"I don't know how you can stand it," he complained. "I'm not used to these long hops, yet they don't seem to affect you at all."

"I'm in a hurry," Caleb said simply. He stared morosely at the rows of blank faced dials before him, trying to curb his mounting impatience. Dimly he could see his own reflection in the polished plastic of the panel; the broad strong features, the high cheekbones, prominent nose and narrow eyes of a man who had lived violently and had seen much. Black hair swept back from a high forehead—sharply peaked, it looked like a closely-fitting cap of glistening jet. It matched the colour of his eyes, framed by surprisingly delicate brows. Lines of character were stamped deep into the flesh, and a thin scar traced a path across one cheek. He was not a handsome man, but he was a man that few forgot. Wilner stared at the swirling greyness shown in the vision-screens. It writhed and coiled, twisting in a peculiar pattern that hurt the eyes and depressed the spirits. He shuddered. "I hate hyperspace. One day we're going to engage the hyper-drive—and never return."

"Maybe," agreed Caleb. "It has happened before, and it could happen again, but not to us."

"What makes you so certain?" Irritation sharpened the astrogator's voice. "How can you be sure? How can anyone be sure?"

Caleb stared at him calmly. "Don't let it get you," he said gently. "You know as well as I do that our engines are synchronized to five decimal places. We're safe enough."

"The big passenger ships synchronize down to eight, and still they get lost." He stared accusingly at Caleb. "They only take short hops, a few hours at a time, and even then they aren't safe. Why should we be?" His voice trembled on the verge of hysteria.

Caleb glared at him, fighting down his own nervous irritation. The opening of the control room door eased the tension, and he grinned at the huge bulk of the man who entered.

"Just in time, Jenner. Wilner's getting jumpy, maybe you can calm him down a little."

Jenner carefully set down the tray he carried, and handed each of them a beaker of steaming coffee. He was a big man, fat, and with a florid face that radiated good humour. He chuckled as he looked at Wilner, and slapped himself on his great paunch.

"You want to eat more, lad, get some meat on those bones of yours; nothing like it for soaking up the sonic from the engines. Why, I could stand this for as long as the ship would run. Haven't you ever noticed that all good engineers are fat?" He chuckled again, and slumped in the one remaining seat.

He grinned at Caleb. "What's the matter with him?"

"Wilner's worried," explained Caleb. "He always is every time we take a hop he sits and gnaws his fingers because he doubts our engines."

"Does he!" The fat engineer glared his disbelief. "With me aboard! With the finest engineer ever to have taken a first degree certificate!" He shook his head in mock horror. "The man must be insane."

"I'm not crazy," snapped Wilner angrily. "It's all very well for you to be so smug, you have something to occupy your mind. All I can do is to sit and wait; sit and listen to the damn sound from your engines, sit and think what would happen to us if something went wrong."

"Steady," warned Caleb. "It's the same for all of us." He turned to the fat engineer. "How's our passenger?"

Jenner shrugged. "Sitting on his bunk working at his figures." He sighed. "I've never seen a man so busy. Ever since we left port he's been hard at it. Who is he?"

"Some professor who wanted a quick passage."

"He seems half mad to me," grunted Jenner. "I've had to warn him twice about getting near the engines. Do you think the sonic is getting him?"

"Can't be helped," Caleb said tersely. "He knew what he was doing. We're not running a passenger service, and if he insisted on shipping with a free trader, then he must expect what he gets. I can't afford the power to break our journey into short hops." He glanced at the instrument panel.

"This hop is almost over anyway, and we should planet-fall shortly afterwards." He rose from the padded chair and stretched to his full height. Like most spacemen, he was slim, not particularly muscular, but with tremendous stamina and lightning-fast reflexes. "Any chance of synchronizing the engines closer than five places?" he asked casually.

Jenner snorted. "Impossible! I know that the passenger services get down to eight, but we can't." He glared at Wilner. "If he had his way we'd sychronize down to twelve—and have no room left for crew or cargo."

"At least we'd get rid of the noise," snapped the astrogator. "It's about time you engineers did something about it anyway."

"Listen to the man!" Jenner sighed, shook his head and began to speak in the tone of voice normally used to a rather dense child.

"In case you've forgotten, the hyper-drive is based on the synchronized relation between three co-axial coils. I won't go into the theory, neither will I waste your time by explaining why it works at all, but if the coils aren't synchronized—it doesn't." Jenner took a cigarette from a crumpled package, lit it, and sent blue smoke pluming towards the grill of the air-conditioning apparatus.

"Now listen. Theoretically it is possible to achieve total synchronization; in practice it's impossible. The temperature of the coils may vary a thousandth part of a degree. There may be a millionth part of a millimetre difference in the metal helices; any one of a hundred things which would destroy the perfect similarity essential for total synchronization. We do the best we can; anything below three decimal places, and the drive will work, above that it won't. We have five places, some ships manage eight and I've heard of one that got down to ten, but that was an experimental laboratory job."

"Very pretty," sneered Wilner. "But what about the noise?"

"A mere by-product." Jenner dragged at his cigarette. "That is where your engineer is worth all you can pay him. Unless the sonic builds into a destroying resonance you are safe. Uncomfortable perhaps, but safe. That's what happened to all the missing ships. The engineer failed either to damp the resonance, or he allowed the harmonics to climb into the ultrasonic region. In the first case the coils would shake themselves to pieces, and the ship would snap back into ordinary space, stranded years from anywhere or the ultrasonic would kill the crew, passengers, and all life aboard. Simple."

"Maybe," Wilner said dubiously. "But do you really believe that all the missing ships had poor engineers? What about the *Jason*? What about the *Starbird*, the *Invincible*, and a dozen other ships? What about all those we don't know about: little traders like us? How many of those have been lost, and who's to know it? If we vanished, would anyone know?" He stared at Caleb. "Well would they?"

"No," admitted Caleb. "We are free traders, hopping from planet to planet, not even sure of our next port of call." Angrily he shrugged. "Enough of such talk. We're in no danger." He glared at the astrogator. "If you fear hyperspace so much why did you come with us? Why did you become an astrogator in the first place? If we're in danger, then it's you who put us there!"

"Steady, Caleb," said Jenner. He dropped one huge hand down upon the captain's arm, forcing him down into his seat. "Don't let the sonic get you. Wilner's all right, he's just jumpy."

In the control room the sound seemed to grow louder; it hummed and quivered, the glass fronts of the instrument dials sending little tinkling sounds across the room. Caleb tensed beneath the big hand of the engineer, then relaxed.

"Maybe there's your answer, Wilner. Maybe the crews of the missing ships couldn't stand the sonic; perhaps it climbed into the ultra range before they knew what was happening." He shuddered. "It would be easy for the passengers and crew to run berserk; their brain-cells ruptured and bleeding from unknown vibration."

"No," said a quiet voice. "No. You are quite mistaken; those ships were not lost through faulty engines."

Startled, the three men looked towards the door.

A man stood there; an old man, stooped, with weak blue eyes and a pale-lined face. He held a sheaf of papers in one hand—and a slender-barrelled needle-gun in the other.

"Professor!" Caleb lunged out of his chair. "Professor Armitage! What are you doing here?"

"Stay where you are!" The stooped figure straightened, the slender barrel of the weapon menacing the tall captain. "I have no wish to harm any of you, but I will shoot if I must."

"What do you want?"

The old professor held out his sheaf of papers.

"I want you to take me to the coordinates I have marked on these papers. I want you to take me there *now*."

"Impossible," Caleb snapped curtly. "All other reasons aside, we cannot change course once in hyperspace."

"Naturally," Armitage agreed. "But you can snap out of hyperspace and realign the ship. Hurry now!" The needle-gun jerked in his hand.

"Give me the papers." Caleb walked steadily towards the old man, one hand outstretched. Automatically the old man held out the sheaf, Caleb reached for them, then suddenly lunged forward. It was childishly simple; against his trained reflexes the old professor didn't stand a chance.

He stood nursing his arm, the gun on the floor at his feet where Caleb's sudden blow had knocked it.

Armitage looked at the weapon, then at the papers in his hand, abruptly all life seemed to drain out of him.

Caleb caught the thin figure in his wiry arms, and gently rested him on the floor. At his gesture, Wilner drew a cup of water from the wall-faucet, dashed it into the lined features. Wearily Armitage looked at them.

"I'm sorry," he said simply. "But it was the only thing left to do."

"Why?" Caleb snapped.

"I have no money left to hire you, and I must get to those coordinates."

"Tell me about it," suggested the captain.

"You have heard of the missing ships? Good. You have heard of the *Invincible*? His weak blue eyes searched their intent faces.

"I have," said Wilner.

"They have found the *Invincible*," Armitage said simply.

"I knew it!" Jenner slapped his thighs. "What did I tell you? The engines broke down, and they entered ordinary space beyond the reach of assistance." He leaned closer to the old man. "Was it the engines?"

"No."

Armitage stared at them, then struggled to a more comfortable position.

"It was not the engines, they were intact when found. Neither was it the ultrasonic." He paused. "There was no trace of any living thing aboard; living or dead. The ship was deserted."

"Impossible!" Caleb snapped his disbelief. "There must have been some traces. The *Invincible* has only been reported missing for the past six months, the emergency stores would have kept them alive for that time."

"The stores had not been touched; the hull had not been punctured, there was no reason for the ship not reaching its destination, no reason—except one."

"And that is?"

"Something happened to that ship; something in hyperspace. Something happened to the passengers and crew; something—or somebody."

In the sudden silence the murmur of the engines droned startlingly loud. Wilner stirred restlessly.

"Piracy?"

"No. As far as we know it is impossible to board a ship in hyperspace; even if it could ever be located."

"What then?"

Armitage drew a deep breath. "I believe that the ship was attacked by creatures native to hyperspace."

"Nonsense!" Caleb rose to his feet and strode impatiently about the narrow confines of the control room. "Hyperspace is a mathematical creation; a closed system formed and maintained by the hyperdrive. It is peculiar to the drive itself; a state inherent in the operation of the engines, and non-existent away from them."

"How do you know?" Armitage struggled to his feet. "What is hyperspace? Do you know? Does anyone? No." He slumped weakly into a chair. "The engines set up a spatial strain; a strain so great that normal space cannot hold it, and so the engines together with their field slip into a peculiar region. In this region the field can exist; and as normal rules no longer apply, speeds faster than that of light are possible. An hour in hyperspace, and you have travelled a light-year in our normal universe."

"We know that," Caleb said impatiently. "What of it?"

"It's a false concept; that's what is wrong."

"It works, and that's good enough for me."

"It works," agreed Armitage. "It works until one day a ship vanishes; any ship, perhaps even your ship."

"What is your theory then?" Caleb glanced at the banked dials and nervously bit his lower lip.

"My theory doesn't matter. What matters is that the crews and passengers of all those missing ships are in need of help. The *Invincible* has been found, minus crew and two hundred passengers. Where are they?"

"Do you know?"

"No," admitted Armitage. "But I hope to find them. I must find them."

"Why?"

"Because where they are the rest may be; the folk from the other missing ships. The *Jason* has been lost for three months; she carried seven crew and five passengers. My daughter was one of the passengers."

"I'm sorry," said Caleb. "But even if I were willing still I couldn't go on this wild search. I am a free-trader plying for trade on the fringe of civilisation. I have neither the time nor the money to waste fuel on a search I know to be useless. I would like to help you, but as you can see it is impossible."

"Please," begged the old man. "I know that there is a chance to save them. Look!" He scrabbled on the floor scooping up his scattered papers. "I have evolved a system of hyperspace mathematics; with it I can plot the probable course of a ship through hyperspace in relation to our normal universe. We can contact the missing ship.

Please help me."

"No."

Armitage slumped in despair, his thin shoulders quivering.

"If humanity doesn't appeal to you, perhaps money would. The *Jason* carried a cargo of urillium worth two billion. It could be yours for the taking."

"Think of it!" Armitage pressed eagerly. "Two billion. A fortune! Think of what you could do with such a sum."

"If it's there," Caleb said drily. "I've heard such tales before."

"You are a free-trader; a gambler, a man willing to take a chance. What better odds could you ask? A trip through hyperspace; a trip such as you make every day, and the chance of a fortune at the end of it. What have you to lose? A few days at the most. What trading would bring you two billion in a few days?"

Wilner licked his thin lips

"It's a chance, Caleb," he urged. "Why not take it?"

"And you, Jenner?" Caleb looked at the fat man.

"What have we to lose?"

Caleb nodded. "How long will this take?" he asked Armitage.

"A week. Perhaps a few days longer." The old man clutched at Caleb's arm. "You won't regret this; I promise that you won't. Help me find my daughter, and I'll make you the richest trader in the Galaxy."

"Thanks." Caleb shook his arm from Armitage's grasp. "I'm capable of earning my own wealth. A week then, and the urillium is mine."

"Yes," breathed the old man. "All I want is my girl."

From the instrument panel a buzzer sounded a strident warning.

CHAPTER 2

THE AUCTION

WITH a quick movement of his hand Caleb silenced the warning buzzer, and slipped into the pilot's chair.

"Watch your engines, Jenner," he snapped. "We're due out of hyperspace."

Tensely he sat before the banked controls, hands resting lightly on the serried levers and buttons. A red lamp flashed, and Caleb grew yet more tense.

Deep within the ship the humped hulk of the hyper-drive engines glistened beneath the tube lights. Emergence from hyperspace was always a chancy business. They could emerge within the heart of a sun; or mere miles from the surface of a planet. Ships had been known to emerge in solid rock, or deep within a sea. Chance played a great part.

They could aim the ship; the astrogator could plot a course, allow for variables and determine transit time, yet they could never be certain. The hyper-drive would be engaged; the ship would be surrounded by the greyness of alien space, and after a predetermined length of time, the drive would be disengaged, and the ship would emerge into normal space. For every hour in hyperspace, a light-year of distance would be travelled; but not always accurately.

Most ships took short hops of a few hours or so, realigning their course and taking no chances. Caleb couldn't do that. He was a free-trader; and time often meant the difference between the profit and loss.

"Stand by for release," he snapped into the intercom. "Four. Three. Two. Now!"

Swiftly his hands darted across the control panel, then hands gripping the firing levers of the atomic rocket engines, he waited.

Within the ship grew a sense of terrible strain. The humming of the hyper-drive lowered in pitch; became a deep shaking throbbing sound, seemed to threaten the very structure of the vessel itself. The ship lurched, twisted, moved in an odd slithering motion utterly alien and indescribable; a movement in strange dimensions incomprehensible to a mind accustomed to a world of three dimensions only.

On the vision screens the greyness seemed to boil; to writhe away in subtle turnings that sent stabs of pain shooting through Caleb's eyes. Savagely he blinked, then returned to his vigil.

A final twist of the labouring ship; and with abrupt suddenness blackness replaced the twisting greyness of hyperspace. A blackness relieved by blazing points of lights, shining steadily through the utter vacuum of outer space. Within the ship all noise died, the tube lights flickered once, and for a moment they felt the ghastly nausea of free fall.

Quickly Caleb sent power jetting from the rocket tubes, with the return of weight; he rapidly scanned the heavens then sank back with a sigh of relief.

"Good astrogation, Wilner." He motioned towards the vision screens. "Not a planet within a million miles, but we're close enough for a quick landing."

Wilner grinned, and wiped sweat from his pallid features. "I can always put a ship right on the nose," he boasted. "Within a million miles you say; and that after a twenty hour hop. I think that I'll ask for a bonus."

He sat back calm and relaxed now that the nerve-jarring harmonics from the hyper-drive had ceased. Caleb leaned across to the intercom.

"What percentage of waste, Jenner?"

"Sixty-five." The engineer grunted. "Not too good, Caleb. One more hop and we'll be out of fuel."

"We're landing as soon as possible. Check the tanks and feeds, we may be in a hurry when we leave."

"No!"

"What?" Caleb spun round in his seat, then relaxed as he saw the old professor. In the tenseness of release from hyperspace he had forgotten the old man.

"You can't land!" Armitage protested feebly. "You made me a promise, you know that you did." He fluttered his papers. "You must take me to these coordinates."

"After we have made planet fall," Caleb said abruptly.

"But we haven't time. Remember the urillium, two billion just waiting to be found."

"I don't care if it is twenty billion." Caleb forced himself to be calm. "We haven't fuel for the journey and I must sell my cargo before I can pay for more. I'm not wasting time, on the contrary, I must beat the official courier to Lyridius IV. If I don't, then the stuff I'm carrying won't be worth its weight in dirt."

"How's that, Caleb?" Jenner had returned to the control room wiping his big hands free of oil and grease.

"I bought a load of coryphil essence at our last planet fall; I got it cheap because a synthetic product has been perfected which is ten per cent better than pure coryphil and only a tenth of the price. If I can beat the courier to Lyrdius then I can sell at a profit; if I don't—" Caleb shrugged.

"I don't understand," said Armitage. "Why is it necessary to beat the courier?"

Caleb sighed. "Listen, Armitage, leave the details of trading to me. You know that there is no other way for news to travel between the stars except by official courier. The Lyrdiums won't know about the drop in price of the coryphil; they won't know until the radio tape has been received and broadcast. I want to sell before that happens."

"But isn't that dishonest?"

Caleb laughed, the scar writhing on his cheek.

"No, just good business." He shrugged. "Anyway who worries about some importer getting caught for a few thousand?"

He glanced at the vision screen, and swung back to face the controls. Clear against the backdrop of space, a planet spun slowly before them. Clouds hid most of the surface yet glimpses of blue and brown could be seen through gaps in the fleecy mantle.

"Lyridius IV, prepare for planet fall." Caleb grinned, and beneath their feet the rockets thundered with fresh surges of power.

It felt strange to feel dirt beneath his feet; to look at a sun shielded by atmosphere, and to see the blue of the sky. Caleb sniffed at the air before entering the field administration building, and grinned at the little knot of loungers.

"Tell them that Caleb the trader is here," he called. "Tell the buyers and the importers of rare and precious things that Caleb has a hundred thousand kilos of coryphil for sale to the highest bidder. A bonus for the man who fetches the buyer."

He grinned as they scuttled off intent on their errand. He would soon see if he had beaten the courier.

A tired official checked his papers and noted the time of his arrival. He looked dispiritedly at the tall trader.

"I heard what you said," he muttered hopefully. "My wife could do with some of that coryphil; she's beginning to get wrinkles. Is it as good as they say it is?"

Caleb stared at him, marvelling as he always did at the insane desire for luxury items on planets that really needed staples.

"It'll make a piece of tripe as smooth as a billiard ball," he reassured. "Clear me quick, and I'll let you have ten kilos."

"Your papers will be ready when you are." The official reached for a stylo. "Ten kilos, you say?"

"Enough for a village," Caleb promised. "Free." He accepted the countersigned papers, and leaned forward, his lips against the official's ear.

"Tell me, have you any news on the *Jason*?"

"The *Jason*?" The man frowned. "Now I remember. A private ship, registered from the home planet and bound for Vega. She vanished into hyperspace three months ago, and hasn't been heard of since."

"Registered on Earth, was she," Caleb murmured. "Who was the owner?"

"A Professor Armitage, John Armitage. His daughter was aboard the ship when it vanished." He looked curiously at the trader. "Why?"

"Nothing, just curiosity." Caleb waved the papers. "Don't forget the coryphil." He strode out into the sunshine.

They were waiting for him, a dozen eager-eyed buyers, their fingers itching to make a quick profit. He grinned at them; each attended by his tout, and gestured towards the glistening hull of his ship.

"Well? Who will buy?"

"How much?" A thin-faced, ferret-eyed man thrust himself forwards.

"Nine hundred thousand."

"Impossible!" The man shook his head, and glanced uneasily at the others. "I'll give you half that."

"Who wants to buy?" Caleb ignored the speaker. "I'm a free-trader, if you don't want what I carry then I'll take it to three. The buyers there are more ready to do business with an honest trader."

"Seven hundred and fifty thousand." A fat man called the offer

"Eight hundred." A third man put forward his bid.

"I'll give nine hundred thousand," said the first man reluctantly. "It'll will ruin me but I'll pay it."

"One million," called the fat man

"One million and ten thousand." The ferret-faced man strode forward and gripped Caleb by the arm. "In cash."

"Done!" Caleb grinned and held out his hand. "It is a pleasure to do business with an honest man. My engineer will break cargo and arrange tests for purity. We can settle the financial details in the administration building."

Impatiently Caleb waited while the coryphil was tested weighed and paid for. He flung a sheaf of notes to the man who had introduced the buyer, then gave the rest to Jenner.

"Fuel up, as much as the tanks will hold. Get food and other stores, we may be away for a long time. And, Jenner."

"Yes?"

"Hurry!"

Jenner winked, and hurried away, yelling orders to the field crew.

Caleb strode about the field trying to quell his fierce impatience. The thunder of rockets from overhead jerked his eyes upward, and he grinned as he recognised the trim lines of the official courier. Gracefully the ship landed, recordings were passed and received, and without a second's unnecessary delay, the little ship shot skywards

In a universe where radio was still confined to the speed of light, hyper-drive courier service was the only way to spread news so that it would not be years out of date. Little ships shuttled back and forth between the star systems carrying the recordings. Once at a star system, the recordings were broadcast over the local radio and TV network; local items of news recorded, and distributed.

News travelled like the ripple in a pool; spreading in wider and wider circles as the centre was left behind. It was a highly integrated method, and it had its weaknesses. Caleb smiled as he thought of the golden chances traders such as he had benefitted from as a result of the slow travel of new market prices.

A yell from the edge of the field drew his attention, and after a quick glance towards his ship, he turned to face a crowd of shouting men.

They were led by the ferret-faced buyer, and Caleb could tell that they were in an ugly mood.

"You crook!" snarled the leader. "You thieving, robbing dog! I want my money back!"

"Steady," warned Caleb. He stood, wide-legged, hands resting lightly on his slender hips and stared coldly at them. "What is the trouble?"

"As if you didn't know," sneered the ferret-faced buyer. "You knew the real price of coryphil. You robbed me. I want my money."

"What is he talking about?" Caleb spoke to the other men milling around him. "What is wrong with the coryphil?"

"Nothing," said the fat man. "Larson here has been sold a pup, and he doesn't like it."

"How do you mean?"

"We've just heard the fresh news. Coryphil has dropped to a tenth of its price. The stuff you sold him is worthless."

"Is it?" Caleb narrowed his eyes. "It is worth just what he paid for it. What's the matter with you people? You're smart men, aren't you? Buyers and sellers with a knowledge of your trade. I'm just a free-trader, I buy and sell in the open market. How am I to blame?"

"You swindled me," accused Larson.

"How is that?" Caleb smiled. "You paid me more than I asked. Am I to blame?"

"He's right," said the fat man. "He asked nine hundred thousand, you bid over a million." He chuckled. "You'll have to stand the loss, Larson." His chuckle broke off into a full-throated laugh.

"That's not good enough," snarled Larson. His eyes darted across the field. "Look, he's refuelled and is ready to blast off. Have you ever heard of a trader leaving without a cargo? I tell you—he deliberately robbed me, and remember it could have been any one of you."

"He's right," growled a man. "We've got to stand together against these crooked traders. I say make him give the money back."

"Do you?" Caleb smiled without humour, the scar on his cheek standing livid against the smooth skin. "How do you propose to do that?"

"I'll show you how," snapped the man. He lunged forward, his big fists swinging. Caleb stepped back, blocked a wild blow, and brought the edge of his stiffened hand hard against the exposed windpipe. With a retching grunt the man fell to the packed dirt of the landing field

"Stand back," warned Caleb. "I'm leaving, and I don't advise anyone to try and stop me."

Deliberately he walked towards his waiting ship. The ferret-faced man watched him, his thin features working in insane anger.

"You swine!" he shrieked. "You robbing swine!" His hand jerked to his belt, and returned weighted with gleaming metal. A yell from the fat man warned Caleb of his danger.

He ducked as the thin streak of searing energy spat from the weapon; threw himself down to avoid a second blast and rolled on the dirt to avoid a third. When he stopped rolling he held a slender-barrelled weapon in his own hand.

The ferret-faced man tried to bear down on the trader, his finger squeezed the firing-stud of his gun, and energy dug into the dirt an inch away from the grim face of his enemy. Caleb sighed, jerked his weapon, pressed the stud

Larson swayed, plucked at his throat, and stared stupidly at the tiny dart in his fingers. His eyes glazed, and slowly he crumpled, the weapon falling from his helpless fingers. Caleb climbed stiffly to his feet.

"He isn't dead," he said coldly. "The dart wasn't lethal, merely anaesthetic. He'll recover in an hour or so." The slender barrel of the needle-gun menaced the crowd.

"I'm going now. If you want to join him, try and stop me."

He backed towards the waiting ship.

CHAPTER 3

RESCUE MISSION

JENNER met him in the vestibule of the airlock. The fat man held a squat-barrelled flare-gun in one big hand, and grunted with relief as Caleb entered the ship.

"I thought that you'd been hit," he gasped. He wiped sweat from his streaming features, and dogged shut the outer door.

"No, that buyer couldn't aim straight to save his life." Caleb looked at the needle-gun in his hand. "Lucky that I had this toy, it slowed them down." He looked about him. "Where's Wilner?"

"In the turret. He thought he'd be useful up there."

Caleb nodded. Like all trading craft, passenger vessels also, the ships carried weapons. The chances of being cast on some undeveloped planet with the resultant danger from wild life, made the simple precaution necessary.

Armitage looked eagerly at them as they entered the control room. "Are we ready to go now?"

"A moment." Caleb switched on the vision screen and stood looking at the clustered group of men on the field. His thin lips twitched, the scar writhing on his smooth cheek.

"Look your last on Lyridius IV," he invited. "After what we've just done, I don't think that they would welcome a return visit."

Wilner joined in the laughter as he entered the control room. "When do we blast off?"

"Now." Caleb slid into the pilot's chair, snapped levers, adjusted verniers, and studied the quivering needles and displays of the banked dials before him.

Sound thundered from the base of the vessel. Flame jetted from the tubes; splashing against the packed dirt of the landing field, sending the grouped men scurrying for safety. They carried the limp figure of Larson with them, and Caleb nodded in quiet satisfaction.

The sound grew louder; deepened into a snarling roar, a throbbing note of sheer power. Gently the ship began to lift. Slowly at first, then with increasing speed they shot into the blue sky. Beneath them the planet began to lose detail; from a flat plain it appeared concave, then convex. It fell behind them like a dwindling ball, the blue of the sky yielded to the star-shot blackness of outer space

Caleb fed power to the thundering tubes until they were far beyond the pull of gravity; until the planet seemed but a point of light among the thousands of others gleaming in the heavens, then, letting the rocket engines idle, he turned to the old scientist. "Where to from here?"

"Look." Armitage thrust his papers at the captain. He was almost trembling with excitement. "I have worked out the coordinates. If you will take us to this sector of space we will be well on our way."

"Give me those." Wilner snatched the papers from the old man, and whistled as he saw the scribbled coordinates

"Anything wrong?" Caleb looked sharply at the astrogator. "How long will it take us?"

"Too long." Wilner snorted in disgust. "These coordinates will take us to the other side of the Galaxy."

"No," protested Armitage. "You haven't read the figures correctly."

"Wait a moment." Caleb reached for the papers. "You told me that the *Jason* has been missing for three months. Now if they were in hyperspace all that time, they would have covered a tremendous distance relative to normal space." He scribbled quick figures on a pad fastened beside the computer.

"They would have travelled more than two thousand light-years. Even if we followed them, we would still be that far behind them." He shook his head. "It's useless even to try."

"No." Armitage clutched at his arm. "You don't understand. I have worked out a new theory of hyperspace, and I know that we can find them. For one thing; I know that they haven't travelled anywhere near as far as you suppose."

Caleb shrugged, and looked distastefully at the old man. "I don't like being sent on a wild goose chase," he said quietly. "I depend on my astrogator to plot my course; not some half-cracked idealist. Before I venture my ship and my crew I must be certain of what I am doing."

"I am certain!" Armitage drew himself up to his full height. "I am not insane," he said with quiet dignity. "I will admit that worry for my daughter has made me a little careless of personal details; that, and other things, but I am wholly sane." He gestured towards the papers. "What you have there is the final result of more than ten years of research; the past three months I have hardly even slept in a desperate race to finish my calculations. I know that I am correct. I know it, and I assure you as a gentleman that you will have no cause to regret aiding me now."

"The urillium?"

"That, and perhaps something more to your advantage."

"Yes?"

"Will you help me, as you promised?"

Caleb shrugged and glanced at the others. They nodded and he grinned at the old man. "What have we to lose?"

"Good." Armitage turned to the listening figure of the astrogator. "I want you to plot the best and quickest course to these coordinates; not the first ones you glanced at but these here. Can you do it?"

"Naturally," Wilner said drily. He took the proffered papers and studied the figures for a moment, frowned then turning to a computer, made a few notations, pressed the final key and studied the figures shown in the windows.

"Well?" Caleb leaned forward intently.

"I can get us there. It'll be a long hop, about fifty hours but it is the best and quickest way."

"Fifty hours!" Jenner shook his head. "That's a long hop, Caleb."

"I can stand it," snapped the trader impatiently. "How about you, Wilner? And you. Armitage?" He grinned at the fat engineer. "I know that you can."

The others nodded.

"Good." Caleb turned to the instrument panel. "Give me the co-ordinates, Wilner. Jenner, you see to your engines, we're going to make this quick."

Delicately he swung the ship with light touches of the controls as Wilner called out the figures. He took his time over the manoeuvre; aligning and realigning until the cross-hairs of the directional telescope were fixed exactly on the great star Wilner was using as a guide. Then he was ready.

"Prepare for freefall," he warned as he cut the rockets. Beneath their feet the muted thunder of the tubes died into silence. Nausea gripped them, and Caleb swallowed repeatedly as his hands darted over the banks of controls.

From the powerful atomic motors, power began to flow into the hyper-drive coils. Rivers of power; power flowing in unimaginable quantities from the destructive heart of the atomic pile. Gradually a feeling of tension built up within the ship; tension caused by the very nature of space itself altering as it could no longer withstand the terrible field created by the power-laden coils of the hyper-drive engines.

The tension grew. The tri-dimensional field forced into being and maintained by sheer energy against the normal rules of space, twisted, spun, and fought to remain static.

Within the ship the tension grew almost unbearable; the very metal of the structure seeming to shift and twist as the field forced it into alien lines. Still the engines poured power into the hyper-drive coils, the field grew still more intense; fought still harder against dissipation. In normal space the field couldn't exist, but powered as it was, it couldn't be dissipated. The solution was simple.

With abrupt suddenness the grey of hyperspace pressed against the vision screens. Gravity returned, and the atomic pile ceased pouring power into the coils. The field was static; to maintain its existence it had forced both itself and all it contained into a region where it was able to exist.

They were on their way.

Caleb wiped sweat from his face and neck, and relaxed in the cushioned softness of the chair. He looked tired, the lines on his face appearing to be etched even deeper than normal. He shivered a little as his skin crawled to the whine of the harmonics from the hyper-drive.

"Satisfied?" he asked Armitage.

"Yes," the old man smiled gratefully. "Tell me, Captain, have you ever thought seriously about hyperspace?"

"Call me Caleb," grunted the trader. "We have no formality on board. Hyperspace? Yes, I've done my share of wondering, but I haven't any new theories."

"Well, Caleb, what do you think happens when you turn on the drive?"

"We enter a region where speeds faster than that of light are possible," Caleb said, impatiently. "I told you all that before."

"I know you did." Armitage murmured. "But often things become much clearer when talked over. Tell me, have you ever thought of using normal rocket drive in hyperspace?"

"I've thought of it," admitted Caleb. "I haven't tried it though."

"Why not?"

"Because we're in a closed field. The exhaust wouldn't be able to escape, and anyway, the reaction would thrust us beyond the field."

"Why would it?" Armitage smiled gently. "You forget that the centre of the field is here within the ship. Obviously then, if you moved the centre, you would move the entire field. However, as you say, the exhaust couldn't escape, pressure would build within the field, and as the pressure increased, so the effective ratio of recoil would decrease; that is supposing the hull could withstand the external pressure."

"Is that the only reason?" Caleb smiled contemptuously. "You forget that we are using ionic rockets. It would take a lot of ions to build an external pressure which the hull couldn't withstand."

"Ions travelling at almost the speed of light," reminded Armitage. "They would be reflected from the field, collide against the hull, penetrate it, and derange all electrical equipment within. You can guess what would happen."

"Chaos," agreed Caleb. "Chaos and certain death for all within."

"Exactly." Armitage smiled and rustled his papers. "We can only get an idea of the nature of hyperspace by using the crudest of analogies. Imagine if you can the universe as being the surface of a sphere. Now if we were to enter deep within that sphere, travel a short distance, and then return to the surface, we would find that we have travelled a far greater distance than we had thought. Do you see what I mean?"

"I think so," Caleb nodded. "Much like a wheel. The nearer to the centre you are, the less distance you need travel to reach a corresponding point on the circumference than if you were on the rim. Is that how you believe hyperspace works?"

"Roughly yes, but remember only very roughly. The universe is composed of far more than the three dimensions we are aware of. A universe of which though we think of it as a flattened, lens-shaped collection of suns and planets; could yet be simply the surface of a sphere, a sphere we can never be truly aware of except via the field of pure mathematics."

"It's feasible," admitted Caleb. "Very feasible, and it would explain a lot."

"Would it explain the missing ships?" Wilner ruffled his thin red hair. "As far as I know the field is self-sustaining, theoretically anyway. We pour fuel into the hyper-drive; the hyper-drive creates the field, and when it is strong enough we enter hyperspace. Once in hyperspace the field needs no more power: there is leakage of course, but for all practical purposes the field will last the majority of hops. When we want to release from hyperspace, we drain the coils into the accumulators, the field collapses; and we snap back into ordinary space." He scratched the top of his head. "Simple. If the field collapses at any time, the ship returns. If the engines break down, the ship still returns. If we want to return normally, we can do so. We lose about half the energy we put into the coils, but we return. That being the case—what happened to the missing ships?"

"I told you once," snapped Jenner. "They returned too far from assistance. I'll take the biggest bet you'd like to lay that those ships are drifting somewhere in space, helpless with only their atomic rocket-drive to reach a planet. Even if they did reach one, it could be uninhabitable, or unsettled—anyone of a thousand things."

"No," said Armitage quietly. "That is not so."

"What is the truth then?"

"I told you that the sphere concept of hyperspace was only a crude analogy. We must use another one to clarify what I want to explain. Imagine our universe to be like the page of a book. Next to it is another page; another co-existent universe, separated from our own, but just as real. Now imagine the region we know as hyperspace to be the space between those pages. Can you see what well might happen? Supposing the hyper-drive threw us too deep into that region? When we released from hyperspace, we might well snap out into that other universe; a universe which may be totally alien to our concepts; or again might be so like ours that we could hardly tell the difference. Now do you see?"

"I see," breathed Caleb. "I hadn't thought of that. If you are correct, it may mean the end of hyper-drive travel."

"But if they did go too far," Wilner protested, "Why couldn't they return the same way?"

Armitage sighed. "I wish it were as simple as that, but I'm afraid it isn't so. The *Invincible* was the first ship to vanish, and that was six months ago. Since then many others have been lost, and nearly all of them in the same region. The coordinates I gave you are taking us to that region; not the region of normal space, but the region on that hypothetical inner sphere where the *Jason*, according to my figures, must have been."

"You suspect something?" Caleb looked hard at the old professor.

"Yes. I can't believe that it was just accident that all those ships vanished so soon after each other, and all in or near the same region. Supposing that there is an adjacent universe; and supposing that the beings of that universe also had hyper-drive? You see?"

Caleb nodded. He shivered and glanced uneasily at the swirling greyness of the vision screens. The subtle murmur from the engines sounded startlingly loud in the sudden hush.

Wilner rubbed a hand across lips that tried not to quiver. "Raiding parties," he breathed.

"Aliens waiting to capture our ships and their crews," gulped Jenner. For once his florid features seemed quite pale.

Armitage nodded. "That is what we have to find out. If I am correct, and I hope that I am not, then our very universe is threatened with invasion."

Caleb stood abruptly from his chair. "Enough of such talk," he snapped. "Jenner, check your engines. Wilner, look at the turret guns. Armitage, you had better get some sleep." He forced himself to grin. "Think of the fortune waiting for us when we find the *Jason*, and then think of how you're going to spend it."

He grinned at them, forcing them to smile in return. Caleb knew how ugly thought could be magnified by the mind deranging sonics from the engines. Crews had gone berserk from brooding over imaginary wrongs and fears.

He waited until they had gone about their duties, then sank wearily into his bunk. He was tired, bone-tired, but his mind was active, and it was a long while before he fell asleep.

CHAPTER 4

ALIEN ATTACK

THE hours dragged as they plunged through the strange grey region of hyperspace. Once Jenner had to pour more power into the coils as leakage threatened to snap them back into normal space. Tempers grew short as the quivering sound from the engines rubbed at their nerves, and even Caleb's iron calm began to desert him.

Armitage was the only one of the four who seemed unaffected by the journey. He stood by the computer, fingers darting over the keyboard as he set up his abstruse equations and complex notations. The answers seemed to please him and he seemed years younger than he had when first he came aboard. Trouble came on the thirty-fifth hour of flight.

Jenner entered the control room, his face serious and almost grey. "We're in trouble," he said shortly.

"What is it?" Caleb spun his chair away from the control board and stared anxiously at the big engineer.

"It's the coils. They're getting out of synchronization, too far for me to do anything about it."

"Is it bad?"

Jenner shrugged. "I can't tell. I've done everything I know, but I can't damp out the harmonics. Haven't you noticed the difference in the sound?"

Caleb bit his lip as he listened. Jenner was right, the sound had lost its smooth murmur, now it alternated between a thin shriek and a deep throb.

"We'll have to snap back into normal space," Caleb decided. "Send Wilner down to me, will you? He's checking the turret guns again."

The astrogator shook his head as he heard the news. "We daren't do it, Caleb," he said. "The course I plotted was through a densely grouped star cluster. The chances are that we'll emerge either in, or far too near one of them."

"We must take the chance," snapped the trader. "Jenner tells me that it's only a matter of hours before the coils will either kill us with ultrasonic, or destroy themselves by their own resonance. Figure the best time to emerge, and do it quick."

"Anything wrong?" Armitage joined them from his position by the computer. He listened to Caleb's terse explanation, and then looked sharply at Jenner. "Maybe there's something that 1 could do. May I try?"

"What could you know of hyper-drive engines?" Jenner snorted his contempt. "It took me ten years of hard study and practical experience before 1 qualified for my certificate. What experience have you had?"

"You have the block frozen, magnetic adjustment type of engine?" Armitage remained calm.

"Yes," agreed Jenner. "What do you know about them?"

"More than a little." Armitage looked at Caleb. "I think that I could help you. May I try?"

Caleb glanced at the fat engineer, then shrugged. "What harm can it do? Take him to the engine room, Jenner, and let him do what he can. I doubt whether he can do much good, but the way that we are situated, any chance is worth taking."

Grumbling softly to himself, the fat engineer led the way to the apparatus-cluttered engine room. The hyper-drive engine, a squat, humped-back structure, gleamed in the light of the overhead tubes. From it came the alternating whine, the sound echoing from the thick metal enclosing the entire engine.

Armitage squatted down beside it, and glanced at the settings of the three verniers.

"I see that you synchronize them by means of an adjustable magnetic field. How do you tell when you are at optimum synchronization?"

Jenner handed the old professor an ordinary stethoscope.

"I listen to the harmonics, and set by ear," he grunted.

"A little risky, isn't it?" Armitage took the instrument and slipped the earpieces into his ears. He fitted the suction cup of the stethoscope to the metal of the engine housing and gestured for silence.

Delicately he moved one of the verniers. Abruptly the sound altered, became a jarring, throbbing, quivering throughout the ship. Hastily Armitage spun the verniers and the sound died to a quiet pulsing.

"Don't try that again," snapped Jenner. He wiped sweat from his glistening features. "You hit a resonance which could have wrecked the coils. Here, let me try."

Armitage gestured him to angry silence as he rested his thin delicate fingers on the controls. Again he adjusted, his hands flickering from one to the other of the verniers. His touch was amazingly light, he barely brushed the knurled rims of the vernier controls, his features intent as he listened to the whining sonics transmitted through the instrument clamped to his ears.

The sound quivered, droned and hummed. It wavered, alternating between a thin keening, and a lower pulsing sound. Sweat glistened on the lined features of the old man as he desperately tried to bring the three coils into close synchronization. Gradually a sense of strain began to build within the ship. Jenner noticed it, and glanced hastily at the bank of dials fastened to the engine room wall. Uneasily he glared at the old professor, opened his mouth to speak, then clapped both hands to the sides of his head—and screamed.

Armitage tore the earpieces from his ears, and desperately twisted a control. Sound burst around them, startlingly loud after the sudden momentary silence. Caleb ran into the engine room.

"What the devil are you doing?" he snapped. A thin trickle of blood ran from his nose and the corners of both eyes.

"He hit the ultrasonic," gasped Jenner. "A few seconds more and he'd have killed us all."

"I'm sorry," apologised Armitage. He touched his blood-stained ears and winced. "I couldn't help it."

"Well?" Caleb grated. "Can you fix it?"

"No." Armitage shook his head. "The coils are beyond normal synchronization, they have been used past their effective life. It means a complete new assembly, the engine as it is cannot be repaired."

"I was afraid of that." Caleb slumped into a chair. "Well, that means the end of our little expedition."

"What do you mean?" Armitage clutched hold of the captain's arm. "We can't give up now, your promise—"

"Did not include expensive repair bills," snapped Caleb. He sighed and spoke more gently. "It's not that I want to call it off, it's just that I haven't money to pay for a new assembly. I'll have to sell the ship, share what cash I can raise, and start again at the beginning." His jet black eyes looked bleak.

"I gambled on being able to make enough to carry us over a thing like this, but I lost. I knew that we had run the engines past their effective life; the ship wasn't new when I bought it." He shrugged.

"Better get ready," warned Jenner. "The coils are draining fast, and we can't wait much longer." He pursed his lips with worry. "I hope that we don't emerge in the middle of a sun."

"Wait!" Armitage glanced hopefully at the big engineer. "Tell me, would it be possible to feed power into the coils at a steady rate?"

Jenner nodded thoughtfully. "Yes. I could fix up a bank of condensers and surge controls. Why?"

"What I propose is risky, and it's taking a chance, but I think that it will work." Armitage snatched paper from his pocket and began to scribble rapid equations. "If you can feed power into the coils at a steady rate of one per cent above the present wasting, and keep it at a constant one per cent, then I believe that we can complete your journey."

"A steady one per cent?" Jenner shook his head doubtfully. "The drainage isn't constant, the control on the power feed must be a variable. We haven't apparatus to do the job, it will have to be a manual affair."

"I know that." Armitage looked at the big engineer. "I can control the synchronization, can you adjust the input variable?"

"For how long?"

"For ten, perhaps twelve hours."

Jenner whistled, then looked shrewdly at the old scientist.

"I can handle the feedboard, but what about the synchronization? You didn't make such a good job of it when you tried last."

"The coils are beyond normal control," explained Armitage. "They have developed eddy currents, and the metal has become to a certain extent crystallized. However if you can run a steady flow of power through them, then I know that I can keep them synchronized within three to five places."

"Wait a minute," snapped Caleb. "There's something wrong here. If you continue to feed one per cent extra power into the hyper-drive coils, what's going to happen?"

"How do you mean?" Jenner looked up from where he busied himself over a mass of wires, leads, and apparatus.

"To enter hyperspace takes a certain amount of power, and when we enter it normally the power is shut off and we continue until such time as more is needed to maintain the field. Now what would happen if we just kept feeding power to the hyper-drive?"

"The field would become more and more intense," replied Jenner. He stared at Armitage, the colour draining from his florid features, "If he's right, then that would take us right into a new universe."

"Exactly," grunted Caleb. He stared at the old professor. "Is that what you want to happen?"

"Finally, yes," admitted Armitage. "But now we have no choice. Unless we can maintain the field we'll snap into ordinary space, and maybe we'll emerge in or near a sun. Do you want to take that chance?" He glanced at the worried features. "This way we can at least get to our destination, and by then we shall he well beyond the danger zone of the thick star cluster. Isn't it worth the chance?"

Reluctantly Caleb nodded. He glanced at the big engineer, then at Wilner who had silently joined them.

"Go ahead," he said, and moved swiftly back to the control room. Wilner joined him, and together they stared at the swirling greyness of hyperspace mirrored in the vision screens.

Time passed. Time that seemed to stretch and drag. The quivering from the engines became a thing to be hated and feared, yet it was a thing which meant life itself. In the engine room, Jenner and Armitage crouched over their machines as if they themselves had become things of metal and plastic.

Armitage leaned against the engine housing, his eyes closed, the stethoscope to his ears. His thin fingers drifted over the triple controls of the verniers and from time to time he made the slight adjustments that kept them all alive.

Jenner had stuffed wadding into his ears, and he sat with his hands resting on dual rheostats, his eyes never shifting from the quivering needles of the indicators before him. The muscles of his hands and forearms screamed with fatigue and a thin trickle of blood flowed from his bitten lips, yet he kept the power flow steady; the power which was sending them deeper and deeper into the unknown realms of hyperspace.

In the control room, Caleb sat stiffly before the dials and levers of the control panel. From time to time he cast a calculating glance at the worried expression on the astrogator's pale features. Above the controls, the vision screen swirled in eye-twisting greyness.

Caleb shuddered and glanced at the chronometer. "How much longer?"

Wilner shifted uncomfortably in his chair. "If Armitage is right, we're almost there."

"Good. What shall we do when we release into normal space?"

"Make for the nearest planet. The rocket-drive is still working, and we can't be too far off the inhabited sector."

Wilner grunted noncommittally, then stared hard at the screen.

"Funny! For a moment I thought that 1 saw something out there." The astrogator laughed self-consciously. "I must be going space-crazy."

Caleb stared at him, then at the grey blankness of the vision screen. It looked as it had done for the past fifty hours: a grey swirling filling the screen without break or alteration. "Imagination," he snapped, and turned away.

Something caught the corner of his vision. Startled, he jerked his head to face the screen, and watched with narrowed eyes. The greyness coiled, seemed to twist upon itself, to thin. He gasped. Beside him he heard the sharp hiss of indrawn breath.

Before them, outlined on the screen in lines of twisting emerald, hung a strange vessel. It was cubical; an oddly distorted cube bristling with truncated cones and topped by slender-pointed rods of shimmering blue. There were no signs of rocket-tubes, and the whole vessel seemed to crawl with a writhing lattice of thin lines of glimmering emerald force.

"My God! What is it?" Wilner seemed half-choked with sheer disbelief.

The clamour of the alarm bell woke Caleb from his daze.

"It's a hyper-ship," he snapped. "One of those Armitage warned us about." He stabbed a button on the intercom and rapped swift instructions.

"Alien ship sighted. Prepare for action!"

"Will they attack?"

"I don't know," snapped Caleb. He glared at the astrogator. "How far away are they?"

"I can't tell. We have no method of comparative measurement. They could be a mile across, or they could be a few feet. They could be within a hundred yards, or they could be at the edge of our radar."

Caleb turned as Jenner and Armitage stumbled into the control room.

"There's your alien, Armitage. What do we do now?"

The old man leaned close to the screen studying the alien shape of the strange vessel.

"We mustn't lose sight of it," he said excitedly. "This is our only chance of finding the *Jason*." He turned to the tall captain. "Can we follow it?"

"Maybe," grunted Caleb. He strode to a locker and pulled out several bundles of metal and fabric. "Here, if we are going visiting I think that we'd better put these on. Do you know how a spacesuit operates?"

"Yes." Armitage pulled on the thick shapeless suit, and carefully sealed the joints. "Do you think that these will be necessary?"

Caleb shrugged, and finished checking his suit.

"Maybe not but I'd rather not take chances Here—he threw a squat-barrelled flare-gun to each of the men—"slip these into your outside holsters."

"I wonder what they are going to do?" Wilner stared at the screen. "They seem to be getting closer."

From one of the pointed rods on the fantastic ship a green light sparkled. It seemed to writhe, to detach itself from the rod, and streak across the space between them. Like a glowing emerald star it twisted through the grey of hyperspace, spun aside as it neared them, then touched their hull.

The ship lurched. From the engine room the sound of the hyperdrive became a shrieking whine. Jenner came stumbling into the control room, his face a twisted mask beneath the plastic of his still open helmet. .

"The coils are being drained of power; we're being dragged out of hyperspace!"

"Good!" snapped Caleb. "That's just what we want."

"You don't understand," wailed Jenner. "The coils aren't being drained as they should be. The flow is in the wrong direction!"

"They are trying to force us into their own universe," said Armitage. He smiled at the worried engineer. "After all isn't that what we wanted?"

The ship lurched again as fresh green flame splashed against the hull.

CHAPTER 5

CRASH LANDING

CALEB stood wide-legged before the control panel, and stared at the strange vessel and at the glimmering specks of emerald flame. Beneath his feet the ship lurched again, and the whine of the engines climbed even higher.

"What are you going to do?" Wilner wiped his face through his open faceplate.

"We must get away from them," snapped Caleb. "We aren't in condition for battle. If they drag us into their own universe, then we are as good as dead."

"How is that?" Armitage turned from his rapt studying of the alien ship.

"You know the state of our engines," snapped Caleb. "We cannot enter hyperspace again in the condition they are in. If the alien does manage to capture us, then how are we ever to return?"

"Can't we blast them?" Wilner took a step towards the gun-turret.

"I doubt it. They seem to be able to shoot through our screen, but our guns can't."

"Then what can we do?"

Caleb slipped into the pilot's chair.

"Jenner! Stand by the engines, pour power into the coils, and stand ready for instant release."

His hands flickered over the controls. Abruptly the rocket drive spat flame. On the screen the strange ship tilted, seemed to slip to one side, green sparks flashing from the truncated cones.

A terrible screaming sound echoed from the engine room, a sound that climbed higher and higher, then abruptly climbed into silence. Pain tore at their nerves as the deadly ultrasonic jarred each cell with lethal vibration. Desperately Caleb fingered the controls. "Get into the turret!" he gasped at Wilner. "Stand ready to blast the alien."

Again the rocket drive spat flame in a futile attempt to avoid the darting speck of emerald fire. A mist of blood obscured his vision and Caleb knew that the ultrasonic had reached a stage where they had scant seconds to live. Frantically he tripped his controls.

The ship twisted. It slithered in directions unguessed; in dimensions unknown to the designers of the vessel. The hull plates tore like paper; for a horrible moment it seemed that the sturdy craft would be turned inside out, then normalcy returned, and with it the sharp hiss of escaping air.

Caleb snapped shut his faceplate and nudged the switch of the suit inter-radio with his chin. A muttered cursing from the receiver told him that the others were still alive, and he stared again at the vision screen.

A huge red ball filled the entire area of the screen A sullen angry mass of glowing fire, flecked with black spots and pitted with great craters. Caleb took one brief glance, then in lightning reflex action his hands tripped over the control board.

The ship spun, and from the orifices of the rocket tubes a glimmering stream of ions lashed at full power. Desperately Caleb advanced the firing levers to their full extent heedless of possible damage, careless of fuel reserves. He had but one immediate concern.

To get away from the sullen ball of the giant sun.

From the gun-turret fire thundered in a torrent of energy as the heavy duty flare-guns sent their charge streaking across the heavens. Again and yet again the triple weapons snarled their defiance, and dimly he heard Wilner's triumphant yell over the radio.

"Got 'em!"

"Destroyed?" Armitage sounded worried.

"No, but I drove them off."

Slowly they drew away from the terrible gravity pull of the giant red star. The ship still quivered with the vibration of the ultrasonic, dampened now, and insulated to the structure of the vessel by the lack of the conducting air, but still dangerous to anyone in contact with the hull.

Caleb bit his lips as he felt the insidious vibration quivering from the metal of the control board. He switched on the automatic pilot and stumbled unevenly through the ship to the engine room.

It was a hopeless mess. Jenner looked up from where he bent over the humped mass of the hyper-drive. "How are we, Caleb?" His voice echoed thinly from the receiver.

"Not too good." Caleb stared at the engines. "How are they?"

"Useless. The coils are fused, the insulation burned and the coolant evaporated." The big engineer kicked disgustedly at the housing. "We'll never be able to use this again."

Wilner joined them, the slight figure of Armitage close behind. His voice sounded thin and strained as he stared at the ruined engines. "So we're under rocket power only now!" He moved towards the control room. "I'd better take a few star sights and find out just where we are.'"

"Right. While you're doing that we'll try and make this ship airtight again. How about it, Jenner? Have we enough spares to patch us up?"

"I doubt it," muttered the engineer. "I'll try and make the control room tight, but I don't know about the rest of the ship. The hull is pretty badly torn." He moved heavily about the engine room collecting items of equipment. A portable welding kit, some flux, hull-patches of various sizes, and a great coil of wire. "I can manage it. Caleb. Armitage can help me, you get back to the controls. If you spot a planet try and land, repairs will be a lot easier."

Caleb nodded, and fought his way back to the pilot's chair. "Any luck yet, Wilner?"

"No." Wilner sounded worried. "I can't seem to spot any recognisable stars and I should be able to because I know in what sector we were due to emerge."

"We twisted about a little," reminded Caleb. "We could have been carried off course."

"Not that much. In any case there wasn't any great red star in the entire sector; and we emerged near one as big as Arcturus. I don't like it."

Caleb grunted, and stared at the vision screens. Behind them the swollen ball of the giant star filled the heavens with sullen menace. Before them was almost total blackness; a few dim specks gleamed where there should have been countess points of brilliant light. He shook his head. He was evidently worried.

"I'll cut the rockets down to a safe minimum," he decided. "It's no good burning fuel until we know where we're going. I'll put us into an orbit about the sun."

Wilner didn't answer; he was busy scanning his star tables. He was still at it when they had finally sealed the hull. Air hissed from the emergency storage tanks, and thankfully they removed the thick and cumbersome spacesuits.

"Any luck yet?"

"No." Wilner shook his head. He seemed very tired and more than a little worried. "I can't find one single recognisable star. I've searched the entire field with the electroscope and spectrograph, and as far as I can see we're in a totally unfamiliar region of space."

"Lost you mean?" Caleb bit his lips. "I don't want to ride you, Wilner, but unless we can planet fall soon we shall be in trouble, serious trouble. The air won't last and the food has been spoiled, Also Jenner tells me that the rockets are damaged; firing them in hyperspace didn't do them any good." He strode across the narrow room.

"Can't you spot anything?"

"If I may make a suggestion?" Armitage said mildly.

"Yes?"

"Perhaps we are no longer lost in our own universe. Perhaps the alien succeeded in drawing us through to their own region; wouldn't that account for the lack of recognisable stars?"

"It would," Caleb admitted grimly.

"The aliens must have originated near this star. It would seem logical to suppose that there is a planet within comparatively easy reach; this sector seems to be devoid of other suns."

"If there is a planet it won't be too easy to find," mused Wilner. "The orbit would have to be a wide one; the gravity pull of that sun must be tremendous, and we can even be sure that we are on the correct plane."

"We must search for it, there is nothing else we can do." Caleb reached for the controls, and halted his hand in mid-air.

"Look," he breathed. "Look!"

A glimmer of emerald light glowed at the edge of the screen. A writhing lattice of twisting lines of green energy. A ship came slowly into view; an oddly-distorted vessel, a vessel with a cubical hull dotted with truncated cones

An alien!

Lights and power died as Caleb rapidly opened circuits.

Tensely they watched the strange ship grow larger in the screen, the shimmering lines of emerald fire sparkling and coiling about the strange hull.

For a moment it seemed as if the ship would strike them, then it had slipped to one side, dwindled in the screen, flickered once—and was gone.

Caleb drew a long shuddering breath. "That just about decides it," he said grimly. "Now we know where we are."

"I've back-plotted its probable course," Wilner muttered. "If it came from a planet, I think that we could find it."

"Good. Let's be on our way."

Wilner looked at Caleb and licked pale lips. "Are you serious?"

"Certainly I'm serious, what else can we do? If we are to ever get back to our own space again, then we must repair the ship. We must find their planet." He laughed tersely. "After all, what choice have we?"

Beneath his hands flame spouted from the orifices of the driving tubes.

It was a small, dark world—the single planet of the giant sun, and it looked as bleak and as forbidding as the entrance of hell itself.

They looked at the small, slowly turning ball, and gasped in the fouling air. The search had taken time; had drained their slender reserves of air and water and fuel. Wilner shuddered as he glanced at the uninviting surface of the strange world. Jenner, like Caleb, registered no emotion; only Armitage seemed to welcome the prospect of landing.

"I knew it!" He tugged at Caleb's sleeve. "Down there we'll find all the lost ships. We'll find the *Jason*, and my daughter." He glanced at the set, features of the tall captain. "We'll find the urillium, too."

"The devil take the urillium," snapped Caleb. "What good is treasure to me? I want a ship. I want hyper-drive engines. I want to get back to where I belong."

He adjusted the controls, listening uneasily to the ragged firing of the labouring rockets.

"We'll orbit once, and study the terrain. Then we'll make a quick landing. Wilner, you stand by the guns, if you spot an alien and you think that they've seen us, blast them to dust. We won't have time for the relaying of orders." He brought out the spacesuits and flare-guns. "Wear these. If we are seen, we may have to land fast, and I don't know if there is an atmosphere."

He waited until they were all dressed in the cumbersome suits.

"Ready? Then action stations, we're going in!"

The rockets snarled in sudden thrusting power.

Before them the alien world blossomed in the screen. It swelled, expanded, became a great ragged ball spinning beneath the plunging vessel. Details leapt into being a great yellow ocean; a thrusting ridge of mountains; a desolate plain. There was only one continent; the rest of the planet was covered by the sullen yellow sea, A single great land mass; a towering ridge of mountains bisecting it into two almost equal halves.

"Look!" Armitage pointed excitedly. "There! A city!"

Caleb eased his hands on the controls, sending the ship soaring upwards towards the dark heavens.

"I saw it," he snapped. "A great pile of black spires. Look for signs of a spaceport." The ship swung closer to the desolate surface.

Across the sea again; across the desolate plain, the soaring mountains, the grim black city.

"Look!" Wilner spluttered in his excitement. "A spaceport!"

It wasn't quite that. In the centre of a sandy waste buildings sprawled their black mass. Strange buildings; spired, squat, rounded and angular, and eye-twisting mixture of odd curves and distorted angles. To one side of the buildings a shimmering helice lifted its inverted mouth towards the black sky. Clustered around the spiral were ships.

Alien ships!

Caleb grunted and tugged at the controls. From the turret Wilner's voice rapped urgently over the inter-suit radio. "They've seen us!"

From the sandy waste ships rose lightly into the air. Glimmering ships with writhing lines, of emerald force twisting over the oddly-shaped hulls. Green fire spat from the tips of slender rods mounted on the truncated cones.

From the turret, triple guns snarled blasting streams of destroying energy. One of the alien vessels lurched; the shimmering pattern of green dissolving beneath the impact of the searing discharge. It wavered, lifted a little, then fell like a stone.

From the desert floor came a soundless gush of exploding emerald flame.

"Got one!"

"Look!" Jenner pointed with a gloved finger. "At the foot of that mountain, see?"

Caleb narrowed his eyes.

"A spaceship! By all the gods, a spaceship!"

Green flame burst around them.

Blood rilled from Caleb's eyes, nose, and mouth. Savagely he shook his head, trying to restore his scattered senses. On the screen green sparks flung towards them, and dimly he could hear the thunder of the turret-guns.

Frantically he threw the ship across the heavens, using every trick of manoeuvre he knew to avoid the green sparks of the alien weapons. In the turret, Wilner fired like a man possessed, sending triple streams of destruction stabbing at the threatening hulls of the alien ships.

He fought them off, but he couldn't do the impossible. Twice the ship trembled to the detonation of the green fire. Twice Caleb, fighting the nausea of imminent destruction, flung the ship free, but it couldn't last.

A splutter from the overdriven rockets warned him, and for a moment the ship fell without power. Then he cut in the emergency landing tubes, threw in every erg of power the tubes would stand, and forced himself to ignore the alien ships.

They were over the mountains. Below he could see the jagged teeth of the upthrust spires; teeth which would rip the hull and smash the vessel as if it were an eggshell.

"They aren't following us," breathed Jenner. "They've stopped at the edge of the mountains."

It was true! The alien vessel no longer followed their twisting path; they hovered over the desert, just where the mountains began, but they still spat their flecks of green fire.

Caleb nodded, tried to jerk the ship out of the path of the green menace, and snarled as the rockets died. Desperately he stabbed at a button.

"Prepare for crash landing!"

The ship shuddered as the first of the green specks detonated against the hull. Within the vessel a thin high shrilling began, echoing from the metal, and resonating from the bulkheads and deck plates. A second detonation: a third. The ship fell. Like a broken bird; the hull ripped and torn, the metal singing with an eerie shrilling, the silver ship tumbled through the thin air. It hit one of the high peaks, hesitated for a moment, then slid down the sloping side of an almost sheer drop.

The sound of its passage echoed through the air, a crashing, grating, slithering sound. It continued for a while, then came a long pause. A muffled clanging, a final distant crash, then silence.

In the thin air the alien vessels hung motionless for a long while. They hovered at the every edge of the soaring mountains, and from the tips of the truncated cones, the slender rods still spat, intermittently, green fire. The flecks of glimmering energy fell among the peaks and chasms, and where they hit, they detonated with a sharp release of green flame. Beneath that flame, rock crumpled to powder, and great cracks appeared in the solid stone. After a long while they went away.

CHAPTER 6

THE BLUE GLOW

THE fire was a handful of glowing embers. The shelter, a lattice of frozen branches hastily erected against the wind. The ship was a broken thing; the hull ripped and torn, the ports shattered, the tubes crushed and twisted. From the turret, the slender fingers of guns pointed forlornly towards the starless sky.

Caleb shivered and held his bandaged hands closer to the fire.

"Wilner," he called. "Warm it up, will you?"

"What?" The astrogator blinked and struggled to his knees. A strip of bloodstained rag accentuated the pallor of his features, the red hair forming a thin halo above the dirty white of the fabric.

"Warm up the fire, will you? I'm perished."

Wilner nodded and reached for the squat-barrelled flare-gun in the holster at his side. He aimed the flare muzzle directly at the fire, and pressed the trigger.

A searing bolt of energy spat from the weapon. The blast hit on and around the embers of the fire, and when it had died, the mass of charcoal glowed.

Jenner grunted, and stared sleepily about him, one hand reaching for his weapon. He winced as his movements sent pain stabbing from his bruised flesh. "What's the matter?"

"Nothing, just warming up the fire."

Jenner sighed and moved painfully towards the brilliant glow.

"For a moment I thought that there might be some excitement. He glanced at the huddled shape of the old professor. "Is he any better?"

"No."

Caleb stared at the silent figure and shook his head

"Five days now since we crashed and he hasn't moved in all that time. I don't like it."

Wilner grunted, staring moodily into the fire.

"It's a miracle that any of us are alive. When we hit I thought that it was all over. Even now I can't see why we weren't all crushed to pulp."

"The suits saved us. That, and the fact that we were all strapped into the acceleration chairs." Caleb glanced towards the ship. "Even then if we hadn't hit a peak and slid down the slope it would have been all up!"

"Here we are, all of us injured in some way, without a ghost of a chance of ever getting back home." Wilner sounded bitter.

"Steady," warned Jenner. The fat engineer shifted carefully as he moved his battered bulk. "We're still alive that's something. We have breathable air, thin and nasty I'll admit, but still breathable. We have water, weapons, and a little food. It could be a lot worse."

"Sure," said Wilner sarcastically, "We have water and a little food, and when that's all gone, then what?" He glared at the huge sun low on the horizon. "It'll be dark soon, this planet has about a ten-day night, and believe me it's going to be cold. I know about that type of sun; it's far too big for much radiation to escape from its gravity field, that's why it looks so red and dark. What are we going to do, then?"

"Get another ship."

Caleb looked at his bandaged hands, flexed them, then began stripping off the dressings. The flesh beneath was red and raw, and had an ugly pulpy appearance. He gritted his teeth against the pain as he forced himself to exercise the muscles. Great beads of sweat shone on his face and neck, and his eyes were narrow slits of glittering jet.

Jenner whistled as he saw the injured hands.

"I didn't guess they were that bad, Caleb. How did it happen?"

"Ultrasonic. I caught it from the controls after we came through." He smeared them with salve and donned the heavy space-gloves. "I can't nurse them any longer, we have work to do."

"You said that we could get another ship," reminded Wilner excitedly. "How? Where?"

"When?" said Jenner.

Caleb grinned faintly, then looked at the silent figure lying close against the flimsy shelter.

"When it's dark and we can move without being seen. We couldn't do anything before, we had to rest, and I was hoping that Armitage would snap out of his coma, but we daren't wait any longer." He looked at the big engineer.

"When we were fighting over the desert, just before we crashed, you saw a spaceship. Could you find it again?"

"Maybe," said Jenner. He frowned. "I only caught a glimpse, it was lying in a little gully past the edge of the mountains. Wrecked, at least it looked like it. What's the plan, Caleb?"

"We must find that ship."

"Why?" said Wilner. "If it's wrecked it will be useless to us, just like our own. We want a ship that can get us back home, not a heap of junk."

"We know that our ship is useless," explained Caleb patiently. "Even the guns can't be used; I want a ship near to the alien spaceport, a ship with workable weapons."

"I see." Jenner laughed with sheer enthusiasm. "Do you think that it'll work?"

"What are you talking about?" Wilner looked at the big engineer. "What's the joke?"

"There's only one place on this planet where we can get another ship," explained Jenner. "The alien spaceport. To get one, we've got to blast our way in and take it by force. That's what we want guns for."

"You're mad!" Wilner glared his contempt. "Three men to raid an alien base to steal a well-guarded ship! It's impossible!"

"Four men," corrected Caleb. "Four men, and we'll do it because we've no choice." He stared coldly at the astrogator.

"I don't get it," grumbled Wilner. "The whole thing is insane enough without worrying about an old man who's as good as dead, anyway. How can we take him with us?"

"Carry him." Caleb glanced at the setting sun. "Time to move!"

Painfully they scrambled to their feet.

From the latticed branches of the shelter they fashioned a rude stretcher; a flimsy thing, but all they could do. Carefully they strapped the slight figure of the old professor firmly to it, supporting his head, and making sure that he was as comfortable as possible. From the wrecked ship they took what articles they could carry: food, water, spare weapons and flare-gun charges.

Caleb stared at the crippled vessel for a long moment; then he shrugged and impatiently gestured them on and upwards.

Scrambling, slipping, sweating beneath the thick insulation of the spacesuits, they climbed up the slope, following the marked trail caused by the downward path of the ship. It was hard work. Caleb led the way; behind him came Jenner supporting one end of the stretcher. The astrogator brought up the rear, slipping and muttering curses as he fought to keep his end of the stretcher level.

The slope grew steeper. Three times Caleb had to blast a hole in the icy rock, anchor himself, and draw the others to him with the ropes. The sun was almost touching the horizon when hours later they reached the peak.

Exhausted, they flung themselves down on the splintered stone, gulping great breaths of the frigid evil air.

"We'll never make it," gasped Wilner. His freckled features looked deathly white and the muscle in his cheek jumped erratically.

Jenner said nothing, grunting as the bruises on his body sent fresh stabs of pain lancing through him.

Caleb looked down at the pale face of the old professor, lifted the thin lid of one eye, then slumped down beside the others. He held his hands out before him, well away from contact with his body. The harsh lines of his features seemed even deeper; he looked strangely old.

Before them tumbled the jagged reaches of the mountain range. A hell of hidden chasms. Ice-covered precipices, narrow paths and riven cracks dropping to the far-off waste of the desert below. From the foot of the towering peaks the sandy waste stretched to the distant horizon, dimly lit by the blood-red rays of the dying sun.

Caleb, who was looking at Jenner, shivered as the frigid wind lashed across his bare features. "Any idea where the ship might be?" he asked.

The big engineer rose on one elbow, then climbed to his feet. From a pouch at his belt he took a pair of binoculars and carefully scanned all the tumbled desolation before him. Finally he shook his head.

"I can't tell. We came in at an odd angle; I should say the ship can only be seen from such a direction, otherwise the aliens would have blasted it."

"You must find it!" Wilner scrambled to his feet and snatched at the glasses. Jenner looked at him for a moment, then joined Caleb beside the stretcher.

"Any improvement?"

"No."

"Do you think that we can manage him?" Jenner jerked his hand at the waste below them. "It's going to be hard enough as it is, if we have to carry him—"

"We can't leave him here alone to die!" Caleb took three rapid steps then returned. "I know what we should do, but I won't leave him. In any case he can be useful to us. Remember how he managed to keep the engines running when they threatened to break down? We may need his help if we're ever to get back home again."

"But what can we do, Caleb? He'll die anyway soon, he's been like this for more than five days now, and still he shows no sign of improvement. Shall we all die because of—"

A yell from Wilner broke off the argument.

"Look! Down there! Something's moving!"

With one quick movement Caleb snatched the glasses from the astrogator, and focused them on the edge of the desert.

"Where?"

"Down by that rock that looks like a dog's head. A little to the right of it. See?"

For a long moment Caleb stood searching the jumbled mass of rock, finally he lowered the glasses.

"See it?"

"No. It must have been your imagination." He handed the glasses back to the engineer. "Let's get moving."

"Wait a bit!" Wilner glowered at the tall captain. "What about you having a go at the stretcher?"

"He can't—" said Jenner, then broke off at Caleb's curt gesture.

"Look at my hands!" Caleb extended his gloved hands towards the pale astrogator. "Go on, take off my glove."

"Never mind," mumbled Wilner. "I'd forgotten about your hands."

"Take it off!"

Reluctantly Wilner peeled off the thick glove. He shuddered at the sight of the raw flesh, oozing blood, pulped as if it had been hammered by a maul. He muttered an apology as lie carefully slid back the glove, and picked up his end of the stretcher.

Together they began the nightmare descent.

The food gave out; the water ran low, and the drugs were exhausted. The sullen ball of the sun had lowered its angry bulk below the horizon; and still they had not reached the bottom of the range. Snow swirled about them; snow caused by the rapidly lowering temperature as the sun no longer warmed the thin air. A freezing wind lashed at them, and they shivered within the thick insulation of their suits even as they sweated from the pain of their injuries.

They jumped and slid down the icy slopes, no longer caring or not whether the stretcher was jarred, Armitage was lucky: wrapped in the depth of his coma, he could feel no pain. They envied him. Caleb slumped down on a narrow ledge, and half fell against the poor shelter of an ice-covered boulder. Blood trickled from his bitten lips.

"We can't go on." Wilner sobbed. He was crying, the tears tracing a path through the dirt on his face. "I can't stand it any longer."

Caleb didn't answer the hysterical astrogator. For a long while they rested in silence, the snow piling up around them, the only sounds those of their laboured breathing.

"I can see a light," Jenner muttered.

Caleb didn't answer.

"Look, Caleb! A light, over there!" Jenner lifted his huge body and pointed with one trembling hand.

"Where?" Wilner scrambled to his feet, eyes blazing hopefully from his thin features.

"There! See?"

The astrogator stood, one hand shielding his eyes from the swirling snow.

"I see it! I see it, Jenner! A blue light."

He shook Caleb. "Wake up, wake up!"

"What is it?" Caleb stirred and fell back against the boulder.

"Shake him. Wilner. Don't let him sleep." The big engineer crawled to where the tall captain lay slumped against the rock.

"Wake up, man. Can't you understand? We've seen a light!" Deliberately he swung his big hand, the force of the blow leaving a red welt on the captain's face.

Caleb stirred, rubbing his stinging cheek, and stared stupidly at them.

"What do you want?" he muttered sleepily.

"There's a light out there. Caleb. A light! Don't you see what it means? Food, warmth, shelter!" Jenner shook him with one big hand.

"Come on, Caleb. Let's get moving."

"Wait."

Caleb stared, staggered to his feet and peered into the swirling darkness. He rubbed the back of his glove over his eyes, then angrily dashed a handful of freezing snow into his face.

For a long moment he stood staring into the night, forcing himself to see beyond the swirling drift of snow.

"I see it," he muttered. "Follow me now, but be careful, we don't know who or what they may be."

Jenner stooped, picked up the end of the stretcher, and yelled at Wilner.

"Come on, Wilner. We've carried him this far, we're not going to leave him now."

Grumbling, the astrogator took up the other end, and together they followed the dim figure of their leader into the unknown jumble of rock ahead.

Carefully Caleb felt his way forward. It was almost impossible to see the pitfalls before them; snow and darkness hid their path. Below, glimmering like a ghostly promise, hovered the mysterious blue glow. It pulsed and wavered, swelling into a comparatively brilliant blaze, then dying to a mere flicker. It moved as if it floated suspended in the thin air; a swaying movement as if it hung from the end of a pendulum, and it wavered in strange, ever-altering shapes.

At one moment it was a ball, then an ovoid, then a triangular glow of misty blue. It was a cold light; a remote colour that seemed to breath suggestions of outer space, and of the depths of ancient glaciers. It skipped; rising and falling, jerking to one side, then returning, swaying and twisting.

"What is it?"

Jenner halted, the stretcher bumping against the backs of his knees.

"I don't know," Caleb said slowly. "I don't like it, it isn't human; somehow it seems alien."

"Come on," snapped Wilner irritably. "Anything is better than freezing to death in this madhouse."

Caleb nodded and moved forward. The glow grew brighter, pulsed into a great circle of blue flame, illuminating for a moment the strained faces of the struggling men.

"Wait!" Caleb stopped and held up one hand. "What was that?"

Faintly through the snow-laden air came a thin echo, an echo of a desperate scream.

From somewhere ahead came the thunder of a flare-gun.

CHAPTER 7

ZENNOR

IT was shocking that sound; shocking with its utter unexpectedness. The last thing they had thought to hear in the vast isolation of this alien world was the sound of a typically human hand weapon, and for a moment Caleb doubted his own senses. The gun thundered again, much nearer this time, and with abrupt caution the tall captain glanced around for shelter. Through the swirling snow he vaguely saw a small gully: a mere crack in the ancient stone. Almost filled with snow, thick with ice, barely more than a scratch on the towering side of the mountain, yet it offered some degree of concealment.

He plunged into it gesturing for the others to follow. Tensely they crouched deep in the snow, crouched and listened.

"What was it?" breathed Jenner. The dull gleam of his flare-gun was almost hidden within the grasp of his great fist.

"A flare-gun," Caleb said softly. "Someone is shooting at something."

"They must be friends," babbled Wilner. "Maybe they are shooting at some of those damn aliens."

"Possibly," agreed Caleb. "But we can't take chances. If we stumble on them unexpectedly they are liable to shoot us in error."

"Listen!" Jenner half rose, the gun steady in his hand, menacing the entrance to the gulley.

From somewhere within the shielding mist of snow a voice snarled curses. An old cracked voice, gasping and wheezing, hysterical and incoherent; the voice of a man half insane with rage and fear. Footsteps grated on ice covered rock, something fell heavily, and the snarling stream of words died into silence.

Metal clinked against rock, and the snarling voice began again, but now the listeners could make our legible words. "Damn you! Damn your rotten stinking slimy souls! Blast you all back to the hell that spawned you! Blast you all!"

The flare-gun thundered again, the report echoing from the confining walls. Again, and yet a third time. Caleb watched the brilliant path of the searing energy and grunted in surprise. "He's shooting at the blue light."

Above their heads the strange glow danced in the air; bobbing and swaying with the ever-changing shape and the pulsing blue luminescence they had seen before. As the thin pencil of energy from the gun stabbed at it, it recoiled, blazed brighter, then hovered again, but this time much further away.

"It doesn't like it," muttered Caleb. The cold blue illuminated the harsh lines of his thin features, and accentuated the hollows of his cheeks.

"You swine!" shrieked the thin voice. "Does that satisfy you? Do you want more? More energy to fill your belly? I'd like to feed you until you burst, you soulless dog!"

The voice died in a fit of coughing, then continued as a low mumble. "Four charges left. Not enough, damn it! God, I was a fool to come out. Four charges, and it won't go until dawn."

"What's he talking about?" Jenner frowned and hefted his gun.

"I think that he means the blue glow. He hasn't enough charges to drive it away."

"Did you hear what he said?" Wilner thrust himself between them. "He said that was a fool to have come out. There must be shelter near here, Caleb. We've got to make him take us to it."

"What shall we do?" Jenner glanced at the hovering blue shape. the glow reflecting off his broad features.

"Blast it," Caleb said softly. "Use two guns each and pour it on. Rapid fire, and don't stop until either it goes or your guns are empty. Ready?"

Jenner grunted and reached for his second gun. He hefted them, eyes glaring at the dancing blue shape. Wilner checked the loading of his two weapons, and nodded.

"Fire!"

Four stabbing blasts of searing heat spat from the flared muzzles. Four brilliant beams of energy drove into the glowing ball of the strange entity hovering overhead. The thunder of the guns rolled in echoes from the walls around them, to be joined by four more, then more, then more again.

Four times they fired with both weapons. Sixteen shafts of destruction plunged into the glimmering figure, and then it was over. The shape recoiled, jerked away, then exploded with a brilliant blaze of blue fire.

The utter blackness of the snow-filled night closed around them.

Caleb blinked his eyes and peered into the darkness

"You there?" he called. "Where are you?"

"Who's that?" The thin voice held startled wonder. "Are you men?"

"Yes. Come over here, we need your help."

Something scrambled over the stone and the light of a handbeam shone directly on them.

"Men! By all the gods of space—men!"

"Help us," begged Caleb. "We need shelter, we're all in."

"Yes. Yes, you are, aren't you?" The voice held wonder. Come with me."

Caleb had a glimpse of a bearded gaunt face, a thin figure dressed m a too large spacesuit; then his strength seemed to drain from his body.

Desperately he forced himself to plod on; to ignore the shrieking agony of his hands, and the utter exhaustion of his body. He reeled, and was dimly aware of Jenner's hand on his arm. He staggered, and stared stupidly at the blood rilling from his gashed cheek. He fell, and had no memory of regaining his feet.

An eternity of endless struggle passed. An eternity of frigid wind and blinding snow. He couldn't feel the rocks beneath his feet. He couldn't feel the bruising of flesh as he stumbled and fell; rose and fell again. He couldn't feel the hull of the rocket when he hit it; he didn't know when he entered, and warm air washed over him. He could not see the blaze of light from the overhead tubelights.

Then he didn't know anything. He lay quietly and wondered at the absence of pain. The soft whine of the air-conditioning apparatus droned through sweet air, and he felt thick padding beneath him. Footsteps echoed from their impact with metal, and he opened his eyes.

Jenner stared down at him.

"Hello, Jenner. Where are we?"

"Caleb!" The big engineer grinned and gripped the captain's

shoulder. "Thank all the gods that you're awake. It's been three days now, and I was getting worried."

Caleb smiled weakly, and stared at the curved metal above his head.

"This must be the ship you saw just before we crashed. It's lucky that we found it."

"Lucky that we met up with Zennor, you mean. We'd never have found it in that snow if he hadn't led us."

"Zennor? Is that the old man?"

"Yes."

"How is Wilner?"

"Asleep. He cracked up just after we found the ship, I had to silence him." Jenner looked at his fist and grinned. "I've kept him drugged since we arrived, he'll be all right when he comes out of it."

"Armitage?"

"Sleeping. Zennor was a doctor once; he treated your hands, and he knows what to do with the old man. The coma has changed to a natural sleep; when he wakes he should be as good as new."

"Good." Caleb swung his long legs from beneath the single cover, and tried to stand. He winced as he gripped the side of the cot, and fell back exhausted.

"Take it easy, man!" Jenner glared at him in a real anger. "We can't do anything for a while. and I'm taking good care of things, If you don't give those hands a chance to heal, then you'll never handle the controls of a ship again, It was blind luck that gangrene never set in."

"You win," Caleb admitted. He rested, listening to the thin whine of the air conditioner. He felt very tired, and it was so warm and so comfortable.

Jenner carefully pulled the cover over the sleeping figure.

* * * *

Zennor leaned back in the padded pilot's seat, and stared hungrily at the three men. He was a shell of a man; a man who seemed to have had the life and youth drained out of him. Little red eyes glared from a tangled mass of beard, and his clothing was a stinking mess.

"I saw your ship crash," he said. "It was sure lucky for me that you were on hand to blast that glow-bug."

"Glow-bug?" Caleb frowned and gingerly flexed his newly healed hands. The skin was red and thin looking, but the ugly pulpiness had gone.

"Yes. That's what I call them. I don't know for sure what they are, but I do know that they can be nasty, very nasty."

"Is that one of the aliens in the ships?"

"No." Zennor shuddered and glanced at the masked ports. "I know what they look like; these are something else."

Caleb nodded, and glanced at Jenner. The big man rose and left the control room; when he returned Wilner was with him.

"Feel better now?" Caleb grinned and motioned towards a chair. "I think that you had better hear this."

The astrogator grunted and rubbed the side of his jaw. He glared at Jenner. but said nothing.

"I was a doctor on a small trader," Zennor commenced. He seemed eager to talk, and Caleb guessed that he had been alone for a long time.

"We were making a short hop on hyper-drive when we spotted one of the alien ships. They fired on us, and the next thing we knew was that we were in this universe, very near this planet. They had some sort of a tractor beam on us and we landed close to that big helice on the plain."

"We saw it," said Caleb.

"Good, then you know what I'm talking about. For some reason I didn't like the look of things and so I didn't leave the ship with the others. All the rest piled out eager to explore, they were armed of course, but it didn't make a bit of difference."

"What happened?"

"The aliens got them." Zennor shuddered. "I don't like to even think about it. The aliens aren't human, Caleb, they're nothing like human. The others didn't have a chance."

"What are they like?"

"I didn't see them clearly—I didn't want to. The crew suddenly collapsed; they were probably gassed, and the next thing I knew that the area around the ship was swarming with aliens. I took one look, and then I blasted off as fast as I could." He noticed the expression on Caleb's face.

"Don't blame me too much," he said defiantly. "If you'd have seen what I saw you would have done the same. They fired on me and damaged the ship; I was lucky to have crashed and still remain alive. I've been here ever since."

"How long is that?"

"About five months. I sealed the hull, and the storage packs provided light and power. I go out sometimes: you found me when I'd gone on one of my exploratory trips." He cackled. "Lucky for me that you did."

"What was that thing we shot?"

"The glow-bug? I don't really know. They drift around the edge of the mountains, and seem to soak up energy. At least they can absorb quite a few flare-gun charges, though if they're hit too often they explode as you saw."

Caleb nodded. "What happened to you, Zennor?"

"Happened to me? What do you mean?"

"You should know—as a doctor that is. What was it made you blast away from the aliens? What was it that ruined your health?"

The bearded features writhed with sudden emotion.

"A glow-bug. The first one I met up with. I told you that they could soak up energy, but that isn't what they really want. One of them caught me on my first trip out; I didn't know what was happening until I was surrounded by a blue glow. I used my flare-gun, and it jerked away from me, but I felt terribly weak. I shot at it until it exploded, and managed to get back to the ship." He laughed mirthlessly.

"When I looked in a mirror I knew what was wrong. I had aged twenty years; the damn thing had sucked the life from me. Do you wonder why I hate them?"

"No," said Caleb. "That I can understand." He leaned towards the wild-eyed man.

"Listen. We all of us want to get back home. Jenner tells me that this ship is useless; the hyper-drive coils are fused, and the engine housing cracked. It happened when you crash-landed. We must get another ship, and from what you tell me the only place is at the aliens' spaceport. Will you help us get one?"

"What!" Zennor rose to his feet and began striding agitatedly about the control room. "You don't know what you're asking. You wouldn't have a chance, not a single ghost of a chance. I've seen them; I've seen their defences and I know." He tugged at his matted beard.

"Why not stay here with me?" he pleaded. "We've got food, warmth, and reasonable comfort. We can get extra flare-gun charges from your ship, and then the glow-bugs couldn't touch us. I tell you that it is the best thing you could do. Your other idea is utterly insane."

"No." Caleb stared coldly at the trembling man. "I'm not going to spend the rest of my life here; and neither are the others. We've got to get a new ship, and you're going to help us."

"I can't!"

"Why not?"

"Because—" Zennor straightened his emaciated body, and dropped one hand casually to the squat weapon in his belt "—I am master here, this is my ship, and you will do as I say."

"You yellow dog!" Wilner sprang to his feet, this thin features writhing with hate and fear. "You want us to keep you company until you die, is that it? To stay and rot in this God-forsaken place, living like animals afraid of our own shadow. No. Do you hear? No. I won't do it!"

"Steady, Wilner," Caleb warned. "That isn't the way." He appealed to the ravaged figure of the half insane doctor. "Why not think it over? We can't do anything until we've rested, and until Armitage has recovered. We can't do anything before the night, and that means another fifteen days. We won't force you, all I ask is that you will think it over."

"It's no good," muttered Zennor. "I can't even think about it. Remember, I've seen the aliens. I know what you'll be up against."

"I don't understand." Caleb shook his head in puzzlement. "As a spaceman you must have seen many forms of life. What is there so terrible about these aliens?"

Zennor tightened his lips, and said nothing.

Caleb sighed. "It isn't only us." he said gently. "There are others to think of, the crews and passengers of other ships. The aliens are a threat to our universe. We must try and stop it; stop it before other ships are lost."

"No."

"If you'd only try!"

"No. I can't do it. I won't."

"As you wish," said Caleb. He rose from the chair and moved towards the sleeping quarters. "I'm going to get some rest. Maybe we'll talk again tomorrow."

"Maybe."

"Goodnight," said Caleb. He hesitated, changed his mind, and left the control room. Zennor sat and glared at the controls.

CHAPTER 8

THE LIFE VAMPIRES

THE long night passed, and the huge ball of the giant sun climbed slowly over the horizon. The snow thawed; releasing its moisture to be sucked up by the dry sand of the desert. Day came, the two hundred and forty-hour day of this strange world, and within the ship tension mounted as health improved. Armitage recovered consciousness.

Caleb sat on the edge of the old scientist's cot, and grinned down at the thin white features. "How do you feel?"

Armitage stared at the curving metal of the hull above his head, then at the unfamiliar furnishings around him.

"1 don't remember," he said bewilderedly. "We were crashing, something struck my head and I was thrown from the shock harness. What happened?"

"This ship is a total wreck. We came over the mountain, and were lucky to find a refuge in this vessel. To get back home we must attack the alien spaceport and capture a new ship. From what Zennor tells me, it won't be easy."

"Zennor?"

"A half-crazed ex-doctor who lives in the wreck." Caleb rose to his feet and strode impatiently about the narrow cabin.

"He has seen the aliens. He escaped from thein with this ship, and crashed it here on the edge of the desert. He could help us a lot, Armitage, but he refuses to even tell us what the aliens are like."

"Why should he do that?"

"I don't know. He sacrificed the other crewmen when he escaped, just went into a panic and biasted off." Caleb clenched his hands.

"We necd what information he has, what they are like, what tbe spaceport is like, a dozen little things be could tell us, but won't. Why won't he talk, Armitage?"

"I don't know." The old man stared at the streaked paint of the hull. "When must you have this information?"

"As soon as possible. We could do without it, but any little thing we can learn about the aliens and the spaceport will be of value. I want to start at the end of daylight, say in another eight days. Will you be fit by then?"

"Yes, I'm not injured, just need feeding up a little." Armitage smiled, then frovvned as he noticed the scar tissue on Caleb's hands.

"What happened to you?"

"Nothing. Nothing serious, that is. I'm all right now."

"And the others?"

"Ready when you are." Caleb turned away from the cot. "We've given you artificial feeding, and ordinary massage, you shouldn't feel too weak. I'll send Zennor in to see you; maybe you can make him cbange his mmd." He smiled and left ths room.

Jenner was waiting for him in the control room. He was joined by Wilner. The astrogator jerked his head towards the engine room.

"Look, Caleb. What are we going to do about Zennor?"

"Why? What's happened?"

"He's locked himself in the enguie room, and we can't get at the tools. Try and get him out, Caleb. We haven't too much time."

"I see." The tall captain rapped on ths metal door, listened a moment, then rapped even louder.

"Zennor! Answer me, Zennor. Caleb here."

"What do you want?"

"Armitage is awake. I'd like you to have a look at him."

"One moment." Scuffling sounds came from behind the door, a metallic clang, and the sound of heavy footsteps. The door swung open.

Zennor blinked at them, his little eyes staring from the mat of his tangled beard. Two flare-guns hung from his belt holsters, and a third bulged beneath his short jacket. Caleb looked at them in surprise.

"Expecting trouble, Zennor?"

"I always expect trouble," snapped the man irritabiy. Deliberaiely he locked the door behind him.

"Why did you do that?"

"Because I don't want your fat engineer tearing my ship apart," snarled Zennor. "I know what's in your minds. You want to dismantle the guns, cut the hull, wreck the ship so that I'll have to go with you.

Well, you're not going to."

"Come and see the old man, will you?" Caleb frowned. "We can talk about that later."

He watched the gaunt figure stride down the passage towards the sick room.

"Do what you can without tools, Jenner. Test for size, check everything you can think of, and prepare packs for each of us. I'll handle Zennor."

"We haven't got much time, Caleb." Jenner rubbed the back of one huge hand over the stubble of his chin. "If we want to dismanth; the guns, weld a portable gun-mount, and fix up some essentiai equipment, we're going to need every minute possible."

"Why don't we just jump on the crazy fool and have done with it?" Wilner glared at the locked door. "I don't fcel safe with that lunatic armed and loose."

"That will be the last resort. While Zennor has information we can use, I want to keep him happy. I still hope to persuade him to come with us. We can use any help we can get."

"A lot of use he will be," grumbled the astrogator.

"Perhaps not very much," agreed Caleb. "But he can carry a load, keep watch, and fire a gun. That's all we need."

He glanced down the passage. "I'll go and see how Armitage is getting on. Do want you can."

The drone of voices halted him just outside the cabin, then cautiously he slipped into the room. Armitage had risen, and Zennor rested at full length on the narrow cot. His eyes were closed, his muscles lax, his breathing deep and steady.

"What's happened?" Caleb whispered.

"I've drugged him," Armitage explained in a normal voice. "He'd left his medical kit in here, and I had time to load a hypodermic. He's under a semi-hypnotic drug, and I intend giving him some neolamin. It may take a little time, but I feel certain that we can clear his memory block and find out what you want to know."

"Good." Caleb stared down at the thin figure, and shook his head.

"Poor devil. I'm not surprised that he went out of his mind." He slipped the guns from their holsters. "Do what you can for him Armitage. I'd like to take him back with us, after all, we owe him our lives."

"Trust me. I'll do the very best I can."

Caleb nodded, felt in the pockets of Zennor's short jacket and removed the keys of the engine room door. A jumble of odds and ends fell out of the pocket; a scrap of paper, a tiny locket, and thin diary and some fragments of tobacco. The tall captain piled them on a ledge beside the cot, thrust the guns into his pockets, and left the room.

Jenner snatched at the keys, and hurried towards the engine room. Caleb slumped into the big pilot's chair and looked tiredly at Wilner. The astrogator fidgeted on the edge of his chair.

"What's the matter, Wilner?"

"Have you looked outside at all?"

"No. Why?"

"Look." Wilner swung one of the port shutters to one side, letting a flood of sullen red lights into the control room. He switched off the tube lights.

"Over there. Do you see it?"

"What?" Caleb joined ths astrogator at the port and stared at the jumble of rocks outside.

"Over there, see?" Wilner pointed, and suddenly Caleb could see what troubled the astrogator.

Surrounding the ship, flickering from almost every point of rock and hovering in the thin air, shone a mist of glowing blue. It altered as they watched, seemsd to coalesce, to knot into individual blobs of pulsating blue flame. Even as they watched several lambent balls of cold blue fire drifted close to the port.

Wilner swung the metal shutter, and looked at Caleb.

"What are we going to do?"

"About the glow-bugs? What can we do? Perhaps they will be gone by the time we are ready to move."

"I don't like it," muttered the astrogator. "I've seen what they did to Zennor, and before we can be ready to move we'll have to work outside."

"Strange that they should be hovering outside," mused Caleb. "Zennor said that they seemed to live on pure energy, probably that is the reason the alien ships don't come past the edge of the desert."

He clenched his hand and brought it down heavily on the control panel.

"I wonder—?"

Wilner caught up with him as he entered the engine room.

"Jenner! Check all power sources. Make sure that there is no leakage in the hull."

"What's the matter, Caleb?"

"We're surrounded by glow-bugs. They may be attracted by an energy leak." He grinned humourlessly. "Zennor may have called his pets to keep us cooped up here."

Jenner stooped over a jumble of apparatus, and snorted disgustedly.

"Here. There's a trickle charge from the batteries. It's connected to the outer hull; we wouldn't feel it through the insulation." Savagdy he jerked a cable from its connection, a splutter of blue sparks snapped from the bared end, and a thin needle on a jury-rigged dial fell to zero.

"The swine!" Wilner glared at the trailing lead. "I'm going to see Zennor about this!"

"Wait." called Caleb. "Wait, Wilner. Zennor is—"

A shriek of terrible fear echoed throughout the ship. A cry tom from the very soul of a man faced with something too ghastly to be born. It rang from the metal of the deckplates and hull. It quivered from the insulation, and seemed to hang suspended in the very air.

"God!'" Wilner turned a face deathly pale to the tensed engineer and captain.

"What was that?"

It came again; followed by an incoherent babble of words. Something fell heavily against the passageway. Something scuttled towards the airlock, metal clanged, clanged again, and in the sudden silence a thin voice called, weakly for help.

"That's Armitage!" Caleb lunged for the passageway. "Jenner! Take Wilner and stand by the airlock. Arm yourselves." He ran down the corridor.

Armitage was leaning heavily against the wall of the sick room. A dark bruise marred his temple, and his eyes were wild with fear.

"What's the matter?" Caleb gripped the sagging figure as he shouted the question.

"Zennor!" gasped the old man. "Stop him. He woke frcm the drug, struck me, and ran for the exit porch. Stop him, Caleb! Stop him!"

"Wait here." Caleb almost threw the slight body on to the empty hunk, and ran from the sick room. Jenner looked up as he neared the open port, and shook his head.

"Zennor's out there," he grunted. The big engineer was pale and held a flare-gun ready in each hand.

"Get him," snapped Caleb.

"No, Cateb, we can't!" Wilner was shaking with fear. "The glow-bugs are out thcre, you know what thev did to Zennor. We wouldn't stand a chance."

"He's right," agreed the engineer. "Zennor's as good as dead right now. Look!"

Calcb stared from the open port. Outside, the great swollen bulk of the sun cast strange shadows among the scattered rocks and riven gulleys. Blue fire drifted there; a shifting mass of hovering shapes pulsing and changing, jerking and dancing as the cold blue flame died and blazed in ever-changing patterns.

"Give me your guns."

"No, Caleb, no." Jenner shook his head in stubbom defiance.

"Don't argue with me," snapped Caleb. "I order you to give me your guns."

Reluctantly ths engineer passed them over.

"Good. Now stand watch; if they get too close, then shut the air-lock."

"Don't do it, Caleb," pleaded Wilner. "He called them, now let him get out of it on his own. Why should vou die as well?"

"Cover me." The tall captain glanced at the astrogator, grinned briefly, then plunged into the tumbled waste outside.

Cold bit at him, the bone-numbing cold of dank air, biting wind, and a dying sun. The air was foul, it caught at his throat and sent waves of nausea through his stomach. Tears stung his eyes, and beneath his feet ice made everv step a danger.

"Zennor!" he called. "Zennor, where are you?"

The wind droned around him, and the shadows seemed to move as the glowing blue fire of the shifting shapes danced and hovered around him.

"Zennor. Zennor. Where are vou. Zennor?"

Rock clattered and fell from a gulley to one side. A furtive figure crouched and scuttled a few yards from where Caleb stood waiting.

"Zennor!"

With abrupt suddenness the hovering blue flame swept down. It pulsed, shifted in a bewildering medley of shapes then darted down to engulf the fugitive.

The flare-guns bucked in Caleb's hands. Again, again and then twice more. Blue fire blossomed, blazing like an evil flower and expanding across the sullen sky. Caleb blinked the dancing after-images from his retinas.

"Zennor! To me, man. At once!"

More blue flame. The hovering shapes of the strange entities thickened, changed shapes, and swept down like hungry birds.

Zennor screamed!

Dimly through a haze of blue Caleb could make out his twisted figure. It writhed, jerked and twisted, seemed to sag and grow limp.

Desperately Caleb fired, the fingers of his still sore hands sending stabs of agony shooting up his arms as the squat barrel weapons spat their searing shafts of destruction; but it was useless. The hovering shapes of blue fire drank the energy; drank it, and seemed to welcome it. Blue flame slashed across the sky as a few of them exploded from a surfeit, but the rest hovered even thicker. Sense came to Caleb too late.

Zennor was dead, his body shrunken and looking terribly old. The glow-bugs were all around, more of them seeming to spring from every rock, and the charges of the flare-guns were numbered.

Caleb staggered as his foot slipped on a patch of ice-covered rock, and for a moment his attention was diverted from the menacing shapes. They swooped, and almost touched him, then he recovered and blasted a space clear before him.

A numbness crept over him, a numbness not caused bv the cold. The glowing shapes seemed to have the power to suck the vital energy from a man; to suck it, and leave a lifeless hulk.

Despairingly Caleb measured the distance between him and the safety of the still open airlock. Given sufficient charges for the guns, he had a chance, but he knew that he didn't have enough. Anger surged through him.

"Blast you!" he snarled. "Blast you for the vampires you are. Blast you!"

They swept around him, blue fire sparking and glowing, dancing and jerking, almost hypnotic in their ever-changing form. The numbness grew worse. It was hard to think, hard to see, hard to squeeze the trigsers of his guns. It would be good to lie down, to relax, to enjoy the soft warmth promised by the blue fire. He felt very tired. Thunder echoed around him. The crashing thunder of flare-gun discharges, echoing from the rock and ice, snapping his wavering senses to new alertness. Shafts of searing energy stabbed above him, around him, weaving a pattern of safety, a fire-traced passage to the open airlock.

CHAPTER 9

MOUNTAIN TREK

BLINDLY Caleb staggered through the airlock, almost knocking Wilner and Jenner down as they ceased their continuous fire. Desperately he gestured towards the open port

"Close it!"

He sagged with utter weariness as he watched them shut and secure the double doors. He felt terribly tired, and the pain of his hands sent darts of agony lancing up his arms. Wearily he released his grip on the butts of the flare-guns, the clang as they hit tbe metal deck-plates jerking Jenner's head towards him.

"Caleb!"

"All right now, Jenner. You got to me in time. Thank you, and thank you, too, Wilner. You saved my life."

"Are you all right? Your face, Caleb, you look old. What happened out there? What are they?" Wilner swallowed and looked uneasily at the shut airlock.

Jenner brushed him aside and stared closely into the captain's features. "You fool, Wilner!" he snapped. "You had me worried. It's only fatigue, they didn't actually touch him. A few days of rest and food, and he will be fit again." He sheathed his guns and picked the captain up in his huge arms.

"Don't argue," he said cheerfully. "If you want to talk you can talk lying down. One thing is certain though, we can't move until those things have gone; they seemed to be greedy for destruction, the flare-guns attracted them instead of frightening them away. He snorted. "What can you do with an enemy like that?"

Caleb sighed gratefully as he felt the soft padding of the cot beneath him.

Armitage bent over him, his thin pale features lined and worried. He held a beaker in one hand. "Drink this."

"What is it? Drugs?" Caleb shook his head at Armitage's nod.

"No drugs. We have little time. A rest will do me, and in the meantime you can clear up a problem. What was wrong with Zennor?"

"Is he dead?"

"Yes."

Armitage sighed and sat on the edge of the cot.

"It sounds terrible, I know, but in a way I'm glad. He was mad, Caleb. Hopelessly insane."

"We knew that."

"He was insane with fear. Caleb. With fear."

In the following silence the whirr of the air-conditioner sounded strangely loud. Wilner swallowed.

"What drove him insane?"

"I don't know." Armitage sighed helplessly. "I had him beneath the influence of drugs, and had managed to get him into hypno-reverie. I took him back to just before the landing, he seemed normal enough, and I brought him up the time track. It was as he told us, they landed, the crew left the ship, leaving him behind."

"Well?"

Armitage shrugged. "At the same moment when he had looked through the vision screen and saw the aliens, he snapped out of the reverie. He screamed, jerked from the cot, and headed for the door. I tried to stop him and he struck me. The rest you know."

"So the aliens are still a mystery," mused Caleb. "Could it have been a psychological defence reaction?"

"Perhaps," agreed Armitage. "The guilt complex induced by his cowardice may have caused him to justify his action by imagining something too horrible for his conscious mind to bear. That would make him invent a reason for his action, and the logical reason would naturally be the aliens."

"It fits," said Caleb thoughtfully. "It accounts for his evading any talk of the aliens, and his desire to prevent our going, even though we didn't insist on his accompanying us. He even attracted the glow-bugs to keep us here." He sighed and stretched on the cot. "Whatever it was it alters nothing. We must still attack the spaceport and try to get another ship."

"I'll work on the guns," said Jenner eagerly.

"Good." Caleb grinned at Wilner. "Will you get some supplies together, work on a compass, and try to get a star-sight on the space-port? We will be moving in the dark and I don't want to get lost."

"Leave it to me," promised the astrogator.

"This ship has only token armament: a single light-duty gun in the nose turret. Cut it loose, strip off the sighting gear and automatic loading and trip mechanism. Remember, we have to carry it. Rig an infra-red viewer and also an ultraviolet search-beam and goggles. When you've done all that, weld a drag sled and fashion three sets of harness."

"Four sets," interrupted Armitage.

"Three." Caleb grinned at the old man. "One of us will either be asleep or on watch."

"But what can I do?"

"You have some experience with drugs, haven't you?"

Armitage nodded.

"Can you make some anti-fatigue pills? Neobenzinc, ultra-caffeine, and also some neomorph?"

"NEOMORPH?"

"Yes. There are only four of us, and we daren't take time off for casualties. Neomorph will enable us to forget the pain of wounds and remain active." He glanced at his hands. "I don't want to feel again how I did coming over the mountain."

"Yes. I can do that."

"Good. Now to work, we only have a little time," He swung his legs off the edge of the cot, and staggered a little. Jenner gripped him with one huge hand.

"You rest, Caleb," he ordered. "We know what to do but we can't take a chance on your breaking up later on. Rest now." He winked at Armitage.

"Drink this."

"No." Caleb struggled futilely in the grasp of the big engineer. "Don't. Don't make me drink that. Don't."

He almost choked as the fluid was forced down his throat. Within seconds he was asleep, the lines softening on his strangely old features. Jenner looked down at him, then at Armitage.

"Will he recover? The glow-bug touched him; he doesn't realise it yet but it sapped his life. Will he recover?"

"I think he will," Armitage reassured. "I'll rig up an electronic energen feed, and give him a trickle charge. He couldn't have lost much energy, and what little he did lose must have been electrical. Given time, I could have even restored Zennor." He slapped the big engineer on the shoulder.

"Get on with your work and leave him to me. I'll pull him round."

"You'd better." Sudden anger tinged the engineer's voice. "You brought him here, you and your talk of treasure. It's cost him his ship. It may cost him his life. I hope that you think it's worth it."

"Do you think that is being fair?" Armitage gently shook his head. "I'm not after treasure, and I can lose my life as well as he can, or you can for that matter. I want my daughter. Do you realise what hell I'm going through knowing that she is in the possession of those aliens? Those same aliens the very sight of which drove Zennor insane?" He shook his head.

"You don't have to tell me what I owe Caleb. He is my only chance of ever seeing her again, don't you think that I know that?"

"I'm sorry," Jenner said roughly. "It's just that we've been together for a long time now. I know just what his ship resani; to him; he struggled for a long time to get one of his own. Sorry."

"I understand," smiled Armitage. "Leave him to me."

On the cot Caleb moaned in fitful sleep.

Time passed. The great orb of the sun swung slowly across the heavens, almost filling the entire expanse of leaden sky with its angry hue. Huge though the sun was, yet it did not radiate sufficient heat to melt the patches of ice covering the rock, and Wilner shook his head' as he stared at it.

"No wonder the aliens are raiding our universe," he said to Jenner. "That sun is useless, this planet will freeze solid before very long."

Jenner looked up from where he was busy welding a framework of light alloy struts to form a drag sled.

"It's big enough to warm hell itself," he grumbled.

"Too big. The gravity pull is too great for much radiation to escape. It's an unstable sun. If I lived here I'd want to get away—fast."

"Me too," agreed Jenner. "Let's get down to it, shall we?"

"The glow-bugs have gone, anyway." the astrogator mused. "That's one good thing. I wish the aliens would follow their example."

"Maybe they will," Jenner checked the strength of a weld und thankfully straightened his back. "Perhaps they hibernate or something. It's winter here, isn't it?"

"If you can call it that," agreed the astrogator. "I would not say that the summer is much better."

He sighed and closed the shutter over the port, then frowned at the litter around them. The ship looked a wreck. A space had been ruthlessly cleared and bulkheads cut away. The turret gun, stripped of all unessentials, rested on a swivel mount, the screens of the mfrared and ultraviolet viewing apparatus mounted to either side of the slender barrel. A heap of charges for the gun lay to one side.

"How many do you think that we can carry?"

"What, the charges?" Jenner shrugged. "Not very many. A couple of dozen or so, maybe a few more. Why?"

"Is it worth taking the gun at all for so few shots?"

"Ask Caleb. Personally I'd feel a lot happier if we had a full battery of them, the hand weapons haven't been of much use so far."

"But the aliens aren't glow-bugs," protested Wilner. "Once clear of the mountains we may never need tbe big gun."

"Without it we may never get clear of the rocks," reminded Jenner. "How do you know the aliens aren't the same anyway? Maybe they are based on the same principle. Perhaps the glow-bugs are the savages of this world. How can we know?"

Wilner shrugged. He didn't look too happy.

Caleb joined them when the sun had almost touchcd the far horizon. He looked fit, the sagging lines of premature age had vanished from his features and his hair had regained its glistening blackness. Rapldly he checked ths equipment and nodded his satisfaction.

"Good. You seem to have thought of everything." He stared at the setting sun. "I'd like to make a start as soon as possible. I want to get away from these rocks while it is still light, a slip now could wreck all our plans. How soon could you all be ready?"

"I'm ready now." Jenner flexed his big hands and squared his broad shoulders. "How about you, Wilner?"

"The quicker I get away from here the bettcr," agreed the astrogator. "What about the old man?"

"Armitage? He's packing up some personal medical supplies—anti-fatigue and anti-pain pills. Concentrated vita-tablets, and other things that may he useful. We'll all carry our own supplies so that if by any chance we're separated, we won't be helpless."

"What personal equipment, Caleb?" Jenner glanced at the drag sled. "This won't be able to carry much more than the gun and charges."

"Regulation space-gear and spacesuits. With those we can eat, drink, fight and even sleep for a while sealed off from the outer air. Four fiare-guns each and all the spare charges we can carry. Armitage will be in charge of spare vita-tablets and medical supplies. He'll also carry a lumi-gun, we may need plenty of light and need it fast. The rest of us will pull the sled and carry any gear we can't manage to transport. Any suggestions?"

"If attacked, what is the drill for gun operation?"

"Trust you to think of that, Wilner." Caleb grinned and nodded his satisfaction. "You will be gunner with Jenner as your number two. Armitage will be look-out, and I'll be either nuruber three on the gun, or local guard as needed." He looked at the little group. "Any other suggestions? No? Then assemble fully equipped here in thirty ininutes. I suggest that we all eat and drink as much as possible in the time remaining."

He grinned at them, then turned away. His footsteps rang on the metal of the deckplates, echoed softly from the bulkheads, then died away.

Jenner chuckled and set to work.

It wasn't too hard to cut away the hull, it was almost easy to drag the heavily laden sled from the ship, along the gully and down the ice-covered rock. The hard part came later, when they had left the ship far behind. It took the form of narrow winding trails, splintered masses of upthrust rock, hidden crevices where a single slip would have thrown them all to certain death. Roped together, spurred with the knowledge that there could be no return, that they only had one path left open to follow—the path forward and downward—they plunged on.

It took hours. It took an eternity of effort. It took every scrap of strength from the four of them; and it took a little rnore than they had to give. It took the artificial stimulus of drugs, and the nerve-sapping strength of chemical energy, but they did it, and reached the edge of the desert.

Staggering with utter exhaustion, the bulky figures of men in spacesuits left the tangle of rock behind them. The gritty sand of the desert dragged at their feet, pulling them with invisible fingers, forcing them to march with an exaggerated upward motion of the knees. The ropes of the sled tugged at aching shoulders; but the sled ran on its broad runners and progress was easier than ii had been since leaving the ship.

Caleb called for a halt, and thankfully relaxed on the coarse sand.

"I want to get further away from the edge of the mountains before we rest," he announced. "I know that you must be as tired as I am; frankly, I never guessed that the descent would be so hard, but there is still danger from the glow-bugs. All take one of the green pills, relax for ten minutes, and then on your feet."

"Another green pill?" Armitage sounded worried. "Too much of that drug can be dangerous, Caleb. Is it wise?"

"It's necessary," said Caleb, and swallowed his tablet.

The march recommenced. Caleb, Jenner and Wilner dragged the sled. Armitage sat perched on the breech of the gun, binoculars to his eyes, keeping constant watch over the surrounding terrain. Time seemed to stop. The great ball of the sun still threw its sullen iight over the horizon, though the giant orb itself was out of sight.

Behind them the towering peaks loomed in ever-increasing grandeur, their summits tinted with glowing red and gold, their bases hidden in misty blue twilight; a twilight deepening into the dark of night as it met the edge of the desert.

Within the deep blue mist brighter flecks of blue shone fitfully, pulsing and wavering, dancing and jerking, but remaining above the tangle of splintered rock comprising the foothills of the mountains.

Armitage watched them for a long while, then lowered the glasses.

"No signs of the glow-bugs leaving the vicinity of the mountains, Caleb."

Caleb stopped, threw off his harness, and thankfully stretched his back.

"We'll camp here. Turn and turn about for watch. Two hours on, six off. Me then Wilner and finally Armitage." He drew a flare-gun. "All sleep now."

"What is it?" snapped the astrogator irritably.

"Close your faceplate. We don't know what may be lurking in the desert, noxious gases, anything. Better play safe."

Wilner snapped shut the transparent plastic rolled on his side, and within seconds was asleep. The others followed his example. Half enviously Caleb watched them for a moment, then commenced his lonely vigil.

With abrupt suddenness it grew dark The black sky, unrelieved by a single glittering point of starlight, seemed to press down on him, and the impulse to turn and stare behind him grew too frequent for comfort.

Acting on suspicion, he snapped on the ultraviolet search beam and stared through the viewing screen. Deliberately he swung the beam and gun round in a full circle, scanning the entire vicinity.

Dimly lit by the invisible U.V. rays, the desert sprang to full view, and in the screen that transposed the ultraviolet down into the normal visual range Caleb could see a world of strange distortion; but a world of utter lifelessness.

Irritably he switched on the intra-red screen. The desert still held plenty of heat from the long day: plenty, that is, to activate the screen. He looked at a scene of dark spots and bright shadows; a picture of temperature differentials, but the results were the same. Nothing.

Time passed, and he woke Jenner, changed guard but sleep did not come easily. He had over-tired his body, forced it beyond the limits of normal endurance with the artificial stimulus of drugs. Later be knew would come a period of lassitude, but now his mind refused to relax. Gradually he drifted into nightmare.

CHAPTER 10

FIGHT FOR LIFE

CALEB woke to the shaking of a hand on his shoulder. Instinctively he rolled from the contact, one hand snatching at one of the holstered flare-guns. Armitage called urgently to him.

"Steady, Caleb. Nothing is wrong, just that my shift is over. Shall I wake the others?"

He had switched on the tiny instrument light in his helmet, and by the faint glow Caleb could see clearly the pale tired features. He snapped on his own light.

"Wait," he said softly. He looked at the chronometer within his helmet, and pursed his lips.

"Later than we should be; probably someone slept a while when on watch, it's hard to blame them."

Sight of Armitage's haggard face crystallised a sudden decision.

"Go to sleep, we'll have another round. We could all do with a good rest, and we may not have the chance later on."

Tiredly he struggled to his feet and stepped across to the gunsled. He felt sick, his stomach burned and his head ached with sheer fatigue. His eyes felt as if lined with grit, and his mouth was parched and his throat sore.

He opened liis faceplate, and snapped off the tiny instrument light. The lash of the bitter wind revived him a little despite the strange taint, and he looked about him with fresh interest. The darkness had deepened until it was impossible to do more than see a few inches before his face. He could dimly make out the huddled figures of his companions and the long bulk of the sled, but aside from that, vision was impossible. He frowned. With such an absence of light, it should not be possible to see even the bodies of the others, yet he could see them like dim blue patches lying on the blackness of the desert sand.

Understanding came at the same time as the wish for a geiger-counter. In some way they were all slightly radioactive. Their bodies, their suits, their very equipment. He could see them by their own emitted light! Such radioactivity usually meant death!

Caleb shook his head. To worry about what couldn't be either understood or altered was a waste of time, but it provided a new and more urgent motive for leaving.

Idly he scanned the surrounding desert with the infra-red and ultraviolet devices. The sand had lost quite a deal of its heat and the infra-red picture was poor. The results were the same however. Nothing was living there.

Tiredly he leaned against the slender barrel of the sled-gun and let the fierce wind lash against his features. He seemed to be staring into a wall of solid blackness; only the dim glow from his suit prevented him from the conviction that he was blind.

Before him, like tiny specks of emerald flame, lights gleamed.

At first he thought that they were a product of overstrained eyes, then he thought that they were near, then he understood.

With desperate haste he aligned the long barrel of the gun directly at the rising motes of brilliant green. Beneath one of the loading handles he made a deep scratch on the wheel mount; another beneath the firing lever, and yet a third from the wheel mount to the body of the sled itself. Then he stared at the burning spots of green.

There were dozens of them. They rose high into the blackness of the sky and flashed away from their point of origin. Caleb judged that they either vanished into sheer height, or travelled away from where he watched. After a while the green sparks died and the solid black returned. Later, he awoke Jenner.

Sleep came more easily to him this time and he thankfully settled himself on the grit of the desert floor. Faintly, through the thick fabric of the suit he could hear the thrum of the wind and the scratching slither as the coarse sand of the desert sifted beneath the blast. Tiredly he closed his eyes and drifted into sleep.

He awoke to the thunder of flare-guns. Something clutched at his leg. Something dragged at an arm. Something scuttled along his body and clicked at the closed plastic of his faceplate. The flare-gun roared again, and in the sudden brilliant light Caleb caught a glimpse of clashing mandibles and spidery legs.

Desperately he jerked his arm, flinging what had held it far into the desert. He kicked, and felt something pulp beneath the blow. With the heavy barrel of a flare-gun he dashed the horrible thing from his faceplate, and staggered to his feet.

Wilner stood against the gun-sled, a gun in each hand and screamed a frantic warning. The guns in his hands spat almost continuous fire, and at each searing blast swollen black bodies puffed into incandescent flame. Caleb joined him, his own guns clearing a path through the glittering tide of swollen spidery shapes.

Jenner was raging around the slight figure of Armitage, protecting the old man with a double barrage of destruction, his heavy boots lashing out at what his guns had missed. Thankfully Caleb saw the old man stumble to his feet, and with Jenner make for the sled.

"One on each side!" yelled Caleb. "Spread your fire. Armitage! Get on the sled and fire the lumi-gun!"

A fresh wave of spider things rushed at him, and desperately he aimed his guns. They were big, fantastically so, and yet for all their size they had no great weight. A glistening black body as big as a man's head, wreathed with a tangle of thin long legs. A smaller ball for a head, covered with bristles and bearing a massive pair of mandibles dripping with green ichor. The entire creature covered with black chitin, and darting about with incredible speed and aggressiveness. They looked a little like spiders; and acted like fighting ants.

The desert seemed to be covered with them.

Light sprang into life far above them. A great blossom of brilliant luminescence expanding, illuminating the entire desert for miles around. It threw into brilliant relief the men, the sled, and the glittering black tide of the attacking creatures.

"God!" Wilner sagged against the gun-sled. "There are millions of them!"

"Keep firing!" snapped Caleb. "Jenner, can the big gun be adjusted for dispersed short-range fire?"

"Yes," grunted the big engineer. He slipped an empty gun into a holster and drew another. "I can adjust the nozzle to disperse the charge. Shall I do it?"

"Yes." Caleb kicked savagely at a rushing black shape. "Wilner, get on the sled. Armitage, keep us supplied with light. All of you keep off the ground. Get to work, Jenner. We'll cover you, but hurry man. Hurry!"

A fresh tide of black insects boiled out of the desert around them.

Aside from the click of chitin and the dry rustling of thin legs against the gritty sand of the desert, they were soundless.

Caleb incinerated a whole group of them with a single blast, and watched with interest the activities of those nearest to the shattered bodies.

"Look," he said. "They're dragging the dead and injured away. Like ants, or rather like wolves. Crazed with hunger they will eat their own dead and helplessly wounded."

"How does that help us?" snapped Wilner nervously. His fingers shook as he thrust fresh cartridges into his empty guns. "We'll never be able to hold them off, there are too many of them."

Above their heads the brilliant light slowly died. Armitage lifted the squat wide barrel of the lumi-gun and pressed the trigger. A dull thud echoed from the gun and a thick projectile jerked from the barrel. It arced upwards, burst and flared like high noon.

"How many charges left for the gun, Armitage?"

"About twenty; we didn't carry many as we didn't think to use them."

"Twenty." Wilner looked sick. "That gives us about an hour's continuous light. What happens then, Caleb?"

"Jenner will have the gun adjusted long before we run out of lumi charges," reassured Caleb. "When we can use it, we can use the U.V. searchbeam and infra-red screen."

"But what about when we run out of gun charges?"

"We use the flare-guns."

"And after that?"

"We die," snapped the tall captain. "Stop whining, Wilner. We are all in this together; anyway, how did they sneak up on you as they did?"

"How could I see them in the dark?" Wilner cursed as he burnt his fingers on the hot barrel of his weapon. Irritably he thrust it into a holster and drew another. "The first thing I knew was that something grabbed me by the foot. I kicked at it, and something jumped on me. I knocked it down and blasted it. The rest you know."

"It was a near thing." Caleb glanced at Jenner, and directed his fire to a point just beyond the busy engineer. "We are pretty safe up here. We can burn them as they come, and if any do try to jump on the sled, we can kick them off."

"I don't think that they are too dangerous," said Armitage. "They would probably rip through the suits in time, but they're so fragile that a protected man could smash them with his fists and boots."

"A few at a time perhaps," agreed Caleb. "But a man wouldn't stand a chancs against a number of them. They'd smother him, pile on top of him until he couldn't move. Strip the flesh off his bones in a matter of ssconds. Ants can do it, and these things are a lot bigger than ants."

"True," he admitted.

"Save your fire if you can," warned Caleb. "We may have to fight our way to the spaceport, and our charges are limited." He looked impatiently at the big engineer. "How are you going, Jenner?"

"A minute," grunted the big man. "I think—there!" He stepped back and gestursd to Wilner. "It's all yours."

Expertly the astrogator slid into the gun seat and checked the loading.

"Right. Feed me, Jenner, when you're ready?"

Caleb squinted up at the dying light. "Straight ahead, low down, and as parallel to the ground as you can get." He paused. "Fire!"

A ravening blast of energy spouted from the slender barrel. It fanned, dispersed itself into wide flarings of brilliant light, splashing from the sand and searing a broad path. It died, and the click of the breech sounded strangely loud in the sudden silence. Expertly, Wilner spun the controls, and the long barrel shifted in a fifty-degree turn. Again searing destruction flared from the gun; another adjustment, again the stabbing spray of brilliant energy.

Steadily Wilner swung the gun round in a full circle, firing it in a set pattern that covered every immediate foot of the surrounding desert. Finally he slipped from the seat and grunted with quiet satisfaction.

A layer of black ash surrounded them. A dry, seared heap of burnt chitin and incinerated insects. Even as they watched the wind caught at the piled heaps and blew them away. Caleb fired another charge from the lumi-gun.

"Good. Now reload your weapons, restock with spare charges, and let's be on our way."

"Is it safe?" Wilner looked nervously at the blackness beyond the edge of light.

"I think so, in any case we can't sray here." Caleb slapped him on the shoulder. "Good shooting, Wilner. Now I want to realign the gun exactly as it was."

Carefully he moved the long barrel until the scratches he had made on the wheel mount and the sled matched perfectly.

"While on watch I saw a lot of green lights rise from the desert and dart away. I think that they must have been the aliens. I took a sight on them, and n we set our gyro-compasses to that setting, we can march directly on to the spaceport."

"How far were they, Caleb?" Jenner squinted down at his instrument panel as he adjusted his compass.

"Impossible to tell in this darkness, but it is below the horizon. Ready? Then let's get away from here. Armitage, you ride on the sled and be ready with the lumi-gun. Fire a charge at my order, and don't waste any time doing it. Can you do that?"

"Yes, but wouldn't it be better if I kept watch through the U.V. screen?"

Caleb nodded. "You're right. Keep a close forward watch through the screen, and fire a light charge if anything seems about to attack us. Jenner, you take the harness with me. Wilner, you lead about three paces ahead, keep your compass and don't worry about anything else, we'll cover you. All ready? Good. Let's be off."

The straps dragged at his shoulders as Caleb thrust his feet hard against the gritty sand, which threatened to trip him with every step. Behind them, the sled slid along, the slight figure of Armitage crouched over the ultraviolet searchbeam as he carefully scanned the desert. Wilner plunged before them, his feet churning through the coarse grit. Above their heads the light died, and utter darkness closed around them.

It was unnerving, that darkness. Caleb could feel the drag of the straps, hear the tight breathing of Jenner at his side, and the scuff of their boots against the sand. Before them glirnmered the vague blue shimmer of Wilner, but he could see nothing else.

Around them could lurk a thousand enemies, waiting in the night to spring on them and tear them to pieces. A million of the black-bodied spider-like insects; or some other peril equally as grave. They could be marching straight to the edge of a terrible chasm, into a great patch of quicksand, any one of a dozen things could be threatening them from the shielding dark.

Sense came to Caleb as he remembered the invisible ultra-violet searchbeams and the crouching figure of Armitage.

Jenner cleared his throat and spoke softly.

"Did you notice that? Wilner has a blue glow?"

"Yes."

"He didn't have it before we entered the desert. Any idea what could have caused it?"

"I can't be sure," said Caleb. "We've all got it, every piece of equipment shines like that. It must be radioactivity."

"No," Jenner said decisively. "Radioactivity of that strength would have killed us all long before this." He marched for a while in silence.

"It must be something in the desert," he said. "A similar force to that of the glow-bugs. Energy is being sucked from us, all of us, our equipment, too. Slowly, of course, but what we can see is the faint corona discharge." He laughed softly. "A poor explanation, I know, but I'd bet that if we had the correct instruments we could measure a trickle discharge of energy."

Armitage called softly from where he sat on the sled.

"Bear to your right, there is a funnel-shaped depression dead ahead."

Caleb relayed the order to Wilner.

"How big, Armitage?"

"Hard to tell, about three hnndred metres at a guess."

Carefully they skirted the unseen depre.ssion. A strange musty odour welled from the pit, and a peculiar sound echoed faintly through the night; a clicking and rustling as of chitin limbs thrashing in wild confusion.

Caleb shuddered, and gripped the butt of a flare-gun until his muscles ached.

"Past now," called Armitage. "Swing back on course."

"Keep watch to the rear as well as the front," ordered Caleb. "If they were to attack you'd be dead before we could get to you."

"I'll be careful," promised the old man. "Very careful."

The march continued. Hours passed. When they felt weak with tiredness they swallowed an anti-fatigue pill. When hunger gnawed al them, they chewed on concentrates and sipped water from pipes attached to built-in containers. The blackness pressed against over-strained eyes, and their ears sang with the constant effort of listening. Finally Caleb called a halt.

"We'll sleep," he announced. "I'll keep first watch with Armitage, three hours and then we'll call you. That suit you, Jenner? Wilner?"

Wilner grunted and threw himself on to the sand. Jenner cased the ache from his shoulders, took a long drink of water, slipped a flare-gun from its holster, and lay near the astrogator. He slept with the gun in his hand.

Caleb sat next to Armitage on the sled.

"Tired?"

"Yes," admitted the old man. He opened his faceplate and rubbed his eyes, they were sunken and red with constant hours of close watching.

"It won't be long now," said Caleb reassuringly. "We must be very near the spaceport, and then we can eet down to something definite."

He looked curiously at the old man.

"You must think a lot of your daughter."

"I do," said Armitage simply. He hesitated. "My wife died when she was very young, we've grown up together. It must have been an odd life for a young girl. I was always busy and couldn't spare her much time. It sbould have driven her away from me; instead it seemed to have drawn us closer. Now that I am able I want to make things up to her. After this flight we were going to settle down, enter society. I had an idea to give her all the things that she had missed.".

"And both she and your ship vanished."

"Yes." Armitage looked at the tall captain. "You know that the *Jason* is my ship?"

"I checked the registration. Is the urillium yours also?"

"Yes. Insured, of course, but I'd willingly give it all to the man who could return my daughter to me."

Caleb started to speak, then turned his head, listening intently. With one smooth motion he slid into the seat of the sled-gun, snapped on the U.V. searchbeam, and scanned the surrounding desert.

"What?" Armitage jerked the question as he grabbed for the Lumi-gun; he crouched, finger tense on the trigger, as he looked at the intent back of the captain.

"I heard something," breathed Caleb. "A rumble, a deep drone, something. Listen!"

Before them light abruptly flamed into life, green light, brilliant and cold, writhing and twisting lines of emerald energy.

Something gushed from the desert, hung suspended for a moment, then danced away across the horizon. A second gush of lambent flame, a third, then two more. The emerald fire of their passage lit the dcsert for miles around, casting strange shadows. Then they had gone, and the blackness solidified around them. Caleb grunted with satisfaction.

CHAPTER 11

THE GREEN HELIX

THIRTY hours later they stared down at the alien spaceport.

It rested at the bottom of a slight depression in the sandy waste; an eye-twisting maze of odd-shaped buildings dominated by the towering helical construction in the centre.

Caleb stared at it with interest, and turned to Armitage at his side. They lay on the edge of the depression, the sled a little behind them, and Wilner and Jenner keeping watch on the desert they had recently passed over.

"What do you make of the helix?" asked Caleb.

"I'm not too sure," murmured the old man. He narrowed his eyes, and gratefully accepted the binoculars Caleb offered to him.

"It is insulated from the supporting structures, and seems to be composed of a maze of wiring. There are four spirals, four main ones at least, and they weave in mathematical relationship." Armitage lowered the glasses and rubbed at his eyes.

"Any signs of life?" asked Caleb impatiently.

"None."

"Can you see anything of interest? Wait!" He caueht the old man's arm. "Keep your head down, something's happening!"

From one of the hangar-like buildings a ship had drifted. It hovered a few feet from the sand of the floor, and the writhing lines of green which slipped and twisted about the hull were dead and lifeless looking. It glided between two great supports of the helix, seemed to jerk a little, then suddenly lifted until it hovered in the centre of the great spiral.

Emerald flame ripped through the interlaced wires. The four main spirals glowed with a green so intense that it hurt the eyes, and Cabeb dropped the binoculars with a muttered curse. The helical construction crackled with energy, great emerald sparks flashed from point to point, and a deep throbbing filled the air.

Within the helix the ship began glow with vibrant life. The twisting lines of green flame frightened, gleamed brilliantly against the odd-shaped hull, and flowed in writhing convulsions. Abruptly the fire died in the towering spiral, the interlaced wires became dead and metallic looking. The ship hovered for a moment, radiating energy, then with a sigh of displaced air it lifted high into the starless sky and shot away.

Caleb sighed. "It's an energy-charging plant," he breathed. "The aliens have to charge their ships at that central helix." He frowned. "That would mean that they only have a certain amount of energy, an amount that must be constantly lessening. They charge their ships, use them, then have to recharge. Inefficient."

"Perhaps it is all they can do," said Armitage. "After all we used to use accumulators and dry batteries. They had a limited energy life, but they were practicable."

"But not for space flight." Caleb looked thoughtfully at the tremendous helix. "If we were to blast that they would be helpless; their ships grounded." He chuckled.

"How does that help us?" said Armitage. He studied the scene before them with interest. "I wonder how they manage hyper-flight? Perhaps it was an accident, they may have accidentally over-charged one of their ships and the hyper-drive field was created without them being aware of what it was. The ship would vanish, reappearing when the charge had leaked away. On one of those flights they must have seen one of our vessels, captured it, and been fascinated by the engines. Imagine what tremendous advantages our type of engines must have been over theirs. No wonder they continued to attack and capture more vessels."

"Yes," said Caleb, "but that doesn't help us. In which of those buildings do you think our ships are to be found?"

Armitage gestured helplessly.

"I don't know. How can I know? They all look alike to me."

The others had no better idea. They sat crouched on the edge of the depression, and tried to ignore the freezing wind. The green glow from the great helix cast a dim light in the sky and made their shadows stretch before them into tlie darkness of the desert.

"We're here," said Caleb grimly. "It took a long while, and a great deal of hardship. I for one couldn't face the return journey back to the wrecked ship. Can any of you?"

Armitage shook his head. Jenner snorted but said nothing, and Wilner shuddered.

"Now for plans. Have any of you any suggestions as to how we can best enter the spaceport, find one of the vessels, find Armitage's daughter, and get into space?"

"The ships may not be here," protested Wilner. "We know that they have a big city towards the sea. Perhaps they have taken the capturcd ships there."

"I thought of that," admitted Caleb. "I don't believe that they have done. This is a spaceport, equipped to repair and maintain their own vessels. It would be natural for them to have our ships where they could most easily be examined."

"Did you see any of them?" Jenner tried to sound casual.

"No. All we saw was one of their ships enter the helix, receive some sort of energy charge, then shoot upwards and away." He explained his deductions as to the purpose of the helix. "With a few well-placed shots I think that we can ground their fleet; at least we can stop them recharging their ships. It will take a long time to re-paie that helical construction and we can stop their raiding into our univeise tbr a while. That, however, doesn't help us at the moment."

He looked at their blank faces.

"Here is what I propose to do. We can obviously eliminate some of the buildings as being unsuitable, unlikely, or just merely possible. We'll select a few nearest to the edge here and I'll go down and investigate. The rest of you stay up here with the big gun, and if anything goes wrong blast that helix. Jenner, will you readjust the gun for long-range fire? Armitage, you come with me."

Back on the edge of the depression Caleb stared at the oddly-shaped buildings below. "We can discount those at the base of the helix, also those immediately near to it. Those are obviousiy generators and control buildings. They would have had to get the ships under cover, and they wouldn't want to move them too far. Zennor said that they landed in a cleared space." He peered tbrough the glasses.

"If the ships are together, it would have to be a large building," said Amiitage. "And if they were examining the engines, I would suggest that it would be one well awav from the centre."

"It may be the other side," reminded Caleb. He took the glasses from his eyes. "I've spotted a couple that may be the ones we want. In any case we've got to start somewhere and they are as good as any."

He wriggled back from the edge and rejoined Wilner and the big engineer.

"Finished?"

"Just," grunted Jenner. He grinned at Caleb. "When do we go?"

"We?"

"Certainly. Why not? Wilner can handle the aim and Armitage can cover his rear. If there's a fight you'll need me, and anyway two can search more quickly than one."

A gush of brilliant emerald from the spaceport threw everything into sharp relief. Something hissed high into the air, then darted away. Caleb frowned.

"Strange," he said thoughtfully. "Ships keep leaving the spaceport, but none have returned. The place must be almost deserted by now. I've counted over a hundred ships since we started, and there have been a lot more."

"Perhaps they are hibernating," suggested Wilner hopefully. "This planet is entering a pretty severe winter. It's well below freezing point now and it's only just started. Perhaps they evacuate the spaceport and summer on the other hemisphere."

"It could be possible," agreed Armitage. "Wilner may be right."

"I hope that he is," said Caleb feelingly. "If I could be sure of it, I'd wait here for a while, but we daren't waste too much time. Food is low, and we could never live through such a winter, or many more days if it comes to that."

He climbed to his feet and began to check his weapons.

"Ready, Jenner?"

"Ready."

"Good. Align the gun, Wilner, and keep us covered. We shouldn't be too long."

Together, the tall captain and the big engineer entered the alien spaceport. It seemed incredible that they were not seen!

Steadily they walked down the slight slope; the gritty sand dragging at their feet and making progress painfully difficult. On such ground it would be impossible to run or to move with any degree of speed. Caleb licked his lips and took a fresh grip on the butt of his flare-gun. Their lives could depend on the first shot being successful.

The buildings loomed before them, and thankfully Caleb leaned against the strange black material of which it was composed.

Jenner joined him, breathing heavily. Together they stared up at the rim of the dssert, and Caleb lifted a reassuring hand.

"Where shall we start?" whispered Jenner.

"This building. I'll examine it while you cover me. I don't like this silence. I've got the impression of being watched."

The building was empty. The great doors had been slid open, and aside from a thin fiim of sand on the floor it was utterly bare. The next was the same, and the next, and yet a third.

"What do you make of it?" Jenner asked softly.

"These must have been where they kept their ships. Hangars, you might say. The ships have gone and so the bnildings are empty. Come on!"

Cautiously they worked their way deeper into the maze of buildings. They were not all empty; one held great bundles of some soft fabric bound with glistening black metal. Another was filled with oddly-shaped stones and a third held nothing but a single glowing green pool of thick liquid.

"This is getting us nowhere," said Caleb. He paused by a rounded structure and waited for Jenner to join him.

"This part of the spaceport seems to have been abandoned a long while ago. The sand is thick over everything. We must try nearer to the centre."

"Could it be a trap?" Jenner looked nervously around. Under the soft green light from the glowing helix his face looked drawn and pale.

"It could be," admitted Caleb. "Bnt what else can we do? Come on, Jenner. That flare-gun you're holding will kill anything we're likely to meet."

They crept closer among the buildings. A clicking began to echo through the still air. A faint metallic sound, as if somsone were striking two pieces of metal together—or as if two chitin-covered limbs rubbed in irritation.

Cautiously Caleb slid open a door and peered within. The clicking grew louder, became faster, then died avvay. Abruptly Caleb entered the building. A machine stood bolted to a low bench. Apparatus was clustered around it strange apparatus with the eternal black sheen.

Jenner stared at ths machine with amazed disbelief.

"It's the hyper-drive unit from a space-ship!"

Tiny lights flashcd on a board and the gentle clickine commenced again. After a while the clicking died, the lights went out, and there was silence. A new pattern of liehts sprang into life and the clicking started again.

"They're testing it," breathed Jenner in wonder. "But how?"

"Don't ask me," said Caleb. "This isn't like any other place I know. Perhaps they are trying variable fields on it, perhaps anything you like, but we're getting somewhere at last."

The next building was locked. The next held more strange tools. The third building had interior lights; they flashed on as Caleb opened the door. An odour welled towards them, an odour that sent them reeling away from the building. A musty, fetid smell of rot and decay, and slime. It aroused horrible mental images, and desperately they fought the nausea it brought.

The next buiiding held a spaceship. It rested on a thin layer of sand, and even from the door they could see the torn hull and gutted imerior. The metal had been ripped away, exposing the internal mechanisms. Jenner pointed and Caleb nodded in comprehension. The hyper-drive unit was missing.

"This is the one they are examining," Jenner said quietly.

"Yes. Now where are the rest?"

They found them three buildings later. Some had been torn apart. Some had been damaged on landing, and others had gaping holes where the ports and turret should have been.

Three were intact. Caleb trembkd with eagemess as he saw them, and for a moment forgot all thought of caution. He halted by the nearest; a small freighter with pitted tubes and treble guns in its single utrret. A ship very much like the one he had lost.

"Check it, Jenner."

The big engineer disappsared within the ship; he returned after a few minutes looking glum.

"Coils fused, Caleb. It may get off the ground, but that's all it will do."

"Take the next," snapped the tall captain. "Quick!"

This was a sleek-lined passenger ship, a vessel designed to carry few passengers but those few in the height of luxury. Jenner reported after a long while of tinkering within the interior.

"Passable. The engjnes are intact, and as far as I can see, the hyper-drive is still functioning. The atomic pile needs attention, though."

"Good. There aren't any guns, but at least the ship is workable." Caleb turned to stare at the last vessel within the vast hangar. It was the biggest of them all, a beautiful freight-passenger combination. He frowned at tlie lettering on the bow.

"Impossible!" he breathed.

"What is?" Jenner peered at the ship. "It seems a good vessel. Dual turrets with triple guns in each. I know these combination ships. Expensive freight and fast passage."

"Look at the name!" insisted Caleb. "Look at the name!"

"The name?" Jenner took a fevv steps forward. "Why, it's the *Jason*, and with the urillium aboard!"

"Exactly," said Caleb. "Armitage's ship. The *Jason*, and with the urillium aboard!"

"If it's still there," said the big engineer. The sound of his footsteps rang throughout the vast building as he climbed aboard. Caleb followed close behind him.

The treasure was stin there! A great heap of boxes filied the cargo space, each sealed with a red band and stamped with the official recognisance. Urillium! Each box held a small ingot of the valuable metal, the rest of the bulk was comprised of insulation and packing.

Caleb smiled as he saw it, the scar on his cheek writhing with pleasure. He glanced at Jermer. "Check the engines, if they are working we can blast straight out of here with a fortune!"

Eagerly the engineär ran to the humped bulk of the engines. Rapidly his skilful hands darted over the complex controls, and bsneath his manipulations needles jumped on meters, and a faint drone filled the ship.

"All engines working, Caleb," he called. "What next?"

"Get the ship into the open, pick up the others, blast the big helix, and then for outer space." Caleb laughed. "We can overload the hyper-drive field and burst through to our universe. We'll be alive— and I'll have two billion to buy a new ship. We're rich, Jenner! We're rich!"

He stopped laughing and looked strangely at the big engineer.

"Did you hear it?"

"What?"

"Listen."

From outside, from somewhere among the litter of broken ships, came a faint sound. A metallic clicking noise, followed by a peculiar slithering. It stopped, continued for a while, then stopped again.

Jenner looked at the tall captain, he had suddenly gone very white. "The aliens?"

"Maybe." Caleb drew his flare-guns. "Stay in the ship, Jenner. I'm going to see what it is."

It had grown very quiet. Alone in the ship Jenner listened, licked his lips nervously, and walked softly to the exit port. He could see Caleb's tall figure as he moved cautiously between the wrecked vessels. From the wide-open doors the wind swept in a sudden freezing blast, it whined about the vast hangar vibrating from the torn hulls and smashed ports of the damaged ships.

The sound started again, this time much nearer. Caleb paused, turned warily, the flare-guns ready in his hands. He squinted at a patch of shadow, spun sharply at a noise from one of the ships, and shrugged as he recognised it for what it was: a loose fragment of hull rapping against a bulkhead.

"False alarm," he called to the watching engineer. "It was only the wind." He took three steps forward, kicked something soft and yielding, and automatically looked down.

His scream rang throughout the building!

He vomited, shrieked, and tried to run. He couldn't! The thing wrapped around his leg prevented it, and in a state hovering on sheer madness Caleb raised the squat barrel of the flare-gun. Raised it towards his own temple!

Jenner cursed with amazed wonder and ran forward. Sense came to him in time, and he did not look to where Caleb had caught his foot. Deliberately he fired his weapon, the thin pencil of searing energy splashed from the sand covering the floor. Something moved, tried to scuttle away, and met its death in crossed lances of searing destruction.

CHAPTER 12

ESCAPE

CALEB writhed for a moment in the grasp of the big engineer, thcn slowly relaxed. He shuddered, wiped the back of one glovcd hand across his mouth, and stared weakty at Jenner.

"Did you see it?"

"No. I caught a glimpse of something moving and blasted it with both guns. What was it, Caleb? What was it?"

"An alien," Caleb said dully. "Don't ask me about it now. Let's get the others."

He stumbled a little as they retumed to the rim of the spaceport. Wilner raised himself as they approached and looked hopefully at Caleb.

"Did vou find a ship?" He frowned at the captain. "What's the matter with you? Did you find a ship?"

"We found a ship," said Jenner. "Come with us and we'll take you to it. Leave the gun here."

"Did you find my daughter?" Armitage looked anxiously at them.' "Did you see any sign of her?"

"We saw no living human, dead one either for that matter. We found your ship, Armitage. The *Jason* is ready to blast off whenever you're ready."

"I can't go without her," insisted Armitage. "You know that, Caleb." He looked at the tall silent figure of the captain. "What's the matter with you, man? Why don't you answer?"

"He saw an alien," said Jenner. He halted them just before they entered the maze of buildings. "Let me wam you; if you see anything move—blast it. Don't stop to look at it, just burn it to ash. Remember that."

He led them deep into the buildings.

Slowly Caleb came out of his trance-like state. He looked around them, at the silent buildings, and shuddered. Jenner walked beside him.

"Feel better now, Caleb?"

"Yes." He laughed self-consciously. "I suppose that I must appear to be tha very worst of cowardly fools, and if you had seen it, Jenncr. If you had seen those horrible eves—" He broke off with a shudder.

"What was it like?"

"I don't know," said Caleb slowly. "It wasn't the shape that was bad—I'm spaceman enough to have seen strange life-forms before. No, it wasn't that." He paused. "I believe that they are sort of living generators. They emit a high frequency current that in some way acts directly on the emotions. You know how supersonic can rupture the brain cells, how a little of it at the right frequency can cause irritation and depression. Well, the aliens are something like that. I believe that the sight of them triggers the emotional response, and the direct gaze of their eyes is even worse. I felt as if I just had to get away. I couldn't, and so it seemed perfectly natural to kill myself, in that way at least I would escape."

He laughed a little as they walked along.

"I suppose that it is a leftover from their earlier environment. A defence mechanism; if you can scare your enemy away that it as good as killing him. It seems to work particularly well on humans; and it will prevent the two races from ever becoming allies."

"I hope that we don't meet up with more of them," said Jenner looking nervously behind him. "Surely that couldn't have been the only one."

"There can't be many here now," assured Caleb. "The cold must have driven them into warm quarters as Wilner suggested."

"Is this it?" Wilner stared into the vastness of the building housing the ships. "Let's get away from here, I'm gettine nervous."

"As soon as you're ready," agreed Caleb. "All we have to do is to cut away the far wall and we can blast off."

"No."

"No? Why not, Armitage?"

"The contract was to find my daughter. You haven't found her, and we can't go until you do," The old man sounded very firm.

Wilner laughed. "Listen to the old fool," he said scornfully. "He is the cause of our being here. We carry him across a mountain, nearly die of exposure before we reach the desert, fight our way through a mass of things I wouldn't Iike to meet even in a nightmare, find his ship for him—and now he doesn't want to leave. Well, suit yourself Pop. I'm going."

"Hold on, Wilner." Caleb looked at the old man. "I know how you must feel, but believe me, your daushter had no chance. She couid be anywhere, at the city even, or she could have been dead for months. How can we find her?"

"We can look," said the old man with quiet dignity.

"Very well then. While Wilner cuts away the far wall, we'll look for your daughter. If we can't find her here, will you give up the search?"

"We're wasting time," said Armitage. He walked towards the wide doors. Caleb shrusged and joined him.

Incredibly they found the missing humans!

A locked door yielded to the blast from a flare-gun, and a terrible odour welled from the half open panel. Closing their faceplates they entered, and as they did so lights flashed from walls and roof. Caleb stared at a scene from a nightmare!

The walls were lined with narrow bunks, or rather metal trays on each of which rested a human figure. They did not move, their eyes remained closed, and for a moment Caleb thought that they were dead. A gentle rise and fall of their chests signalled differently.

But not for all of them.

Tier after tier consisted of rotting bodies; decayed and eaten. Caleb frowned at them, ran along the serried ranks, and called to the others.

"Armitage! Jenner! Look!"

His finger trembled a little as he pointed to one of the dead figures. Tiny red eyes gleamed at him from beneath an exposed rib-case, and even as they watched something crawled slowly into full view.

Armitage retched, and Jenner wanted to run. The roar of flare-guns jerked him around and he gasped with relief as he saw Caleb deliberately blast into charred ruin yet another of the tiny scuttling shapes.

"They deposit their eggs on living meat," snapped Caleb grimly. "Wasps and other forms of insects do it on Earth; they paralyse their victims with an injection from their stingers and then deposit their eggs on the still-living prey. When the eggs hatch they eat the meat provided."

"Are they all like this?" Jenner swallowed and looked sick.

"No. These must be some of the first to be captured, perhaps the passengers and crew of the *Invincible*." He gestured with his weapons. "Go along the line, burn every living insect you see, and shoot anyone obviously too far gone. I don't think that we will be killong ever one—I imagine that the aliens deposited their eggs in batches, Hurry now!"

The great building began to resound with the thunder of flare-guns. Tiny scuttling things squeaked and ran, only to dissolve into grey ash. Grim-faced, sweating with an insane desire to drop their guns and run, the three men grimly continued with their work of extermination.

It didn't take too long. Armitage leaned against a tier of the narrovv metal bunks and tried not to vomit. He gestured weakly towards the bodies on the shelves behind him.

"These are uninjured, but we'll have to remove the eggs. Look."

He pointed to where a rougb-skinned ovoid rested on the stomach of each individual.

"Remove them, but be quick." Caleb glanced out of the door towards the great helix. "We've made far too much noise and if this is their nursery they will be coming on the run." He glanced at the semed ranks of silent figures. "About fifty. We'll have to take them with us and hope that medical science can do something for them when we get back."

"I'll stay here with Armitage," suggested Jenner. "You go and see how Wilner is getting on with the ship."

Caleb nodded and ran from the building. Behind him the two men commenced a frantic race against lime.

Wilner had finished cutting through the rear wall, and had jock-eyed the ship ready for immediate take-otf. He grinncd as Caleb joined him, and waved a hand towards the ship.

"Bit of luck, Caleb. The *Jason* in perfect condition and with the urillium already loaded. When do we blast?"

"We've found the passengers and crews of the captured ships," explained Caleb hastily. "Most are dead, but we can save about fifty of them. We'll have to dump the cargo to make room."

"What?" Wilner stared his unbelief. "You don't mean that you're going to throw away two billion?"

"Yes."

"But why? Is it because of Armitage? He can't make you do it, he can't make you do anything." Wilner dropped his voice. "Look, Caleb. We're all in this together, you, Jenner and me. Why not just forget Armitage? Why not just leave him here? We can say he died on the journey, anything to explain his death, then the *Jason* will be yours; the *Jason* and two billions in urillium!"

"No."

"But—" Wilner stared in sudden fear at the flare-gun centred on his stomach.

"What is your life worth to you, Wilner?" Caleb's voice sounded as cold as his eyes looked bleak. "It's worth everything you have, or hope to have, your savings and everything you can ever hope to earn from now until the day you die. That is what your life is worth to you." He lifted the flare-gun. "To me your life is worth just the effort needed to squeeze this trigger; the exact cost of a flare-gun charge. Well?"

Wilner stared at the sand-strewn floor.

"There are fifty humans waiting to be saved from a terrible death, Wilner. I can't see them left here because of two b trying to illions in urillium. Do we unload the cargo?"

"Yes," muttered the astrogator. "I'm sorry Caleb but—"

"Let's get to work."

Desperately they threw out the heavy packages of treasure. Fortunateiy the bundles were more bulky than heavy yet each one required their full strengtli to lift. Caleb had thrown open the cargo hatch and assembled the loading conveyors but even then it was hard work, Rapidly the heap of packages grew outside the ship, and finallv the hold was emptv

Carefully they jockeyed the ship near to the nursery building, and then continued the delicate task of loading the hclpless passengers. The bodies were stiff as if from rigor mortis, and the flesh had a cold clammy feel. Each had a red spot on the stomach where the eggs had lain.

Armitage fussed over them with a worried frown as the ship began to fill with the paralysed humans. He began to look even more anxious.

"He's looking for his daughter," whispered Jenner to Caleb as they rested for a moment before entenng the building.

"Maybe she was one of those we had to shoot?" Caleb looked at the old professor. "I hope that he finds her."

The bodies grew less and less until there were only three remaining in the great building. Jenner, Caleb, and the old scientist took one each, Caleb coming last. He looked gently down at the smooth features of a young girl, then carefuliv picked her up in his arms and headed for the almust filled ship. Armitage came running from tbe loading hatch, his face a mask of worry.

"I haven't found her, Caleb! I haven't found her!"

"Steady," warned the tall captain. "I hate to say it, Armitage, but maybe she was one of those we had to burn. They were dead anyway, but we had no time to examine each one." The old man didn't answer, he stared at the srnouth figure cradled in Caleb's arms, then suddenly broke into a fit of crying.

"You've found her, Caleb! My little girl, you've found her."

"Is this your daughter?" Caleb looked down at the young girl in his arms, then tenderly placed her within those of Armitage.

"I'm glad we found her, old man," he said simplv. "Take her aboard, and let's get away from here."

A yell from Jenner jerked his head upwards. He stared at the sullen heavens, then at the great helix. The intricate maze of wiring glowed with sudden energy and a thin whistle began to echo faintly through the thin air.

"Quick!" Caleb leapt aboard and dragged the doors shut behind him. "Prepare for emergency take-off! Aliens above!"

There were three of them plummeting down through the thin air, grecn fiame sparking from their truncated turrets.

Caleb watched them as he buckled himself into the pilot's chair and snapped swift orders.

"Wilner! Get to the guns and blast anything that comes within range. Jenner! Feed the engines. I want as much power in the hyper-drive as the coils will take, and feed it as quick as you can."

"What about Armitage?" called the astrogator as he crawled towards the turret.

"He's busy nursing his daughter. Forget about him for now; the relicf from strain proved too much for him. Ready?"

"Ready!" snapped Wilner.

"Ready!" called Jenner.

"Here we go," said C'aleb, and tugged at the controls.

The ship jerked. Flame spouted from the serried venturis; a pale blue wash of ions moving at almost the speed of light. The vessel shuddered as it slithered along the sand; then it lifted, and acceleration crushed them with the force of many gravities.

Where the ship had lain flame sparkled and the nearby buildings crumpled to dust.

Caleb sat tensed before the vision screens watching the aliens through narrowed eyes. His hands flickered over the complex bank of controls before him, and suddenly the ship veered as emerald fire spat towards them. From the turret came the snarling roar of their answering fire.

One of the enemy ships lurched, leapt upwards, hovered for a moment, then crashed to destruction. A second spun wildly, then swooped for the great helix. Green energy bathed it as it hung suspended within the interwoven spirals, and the twisting lines of emerald energy writhing over the hull took on new life. Recharged, it sprang upwards to join combat.

"Wilner!" called Caleb. "Blast the helix. Now!"

Desperately he swung the ship away from spitting flecks of green flame. The hull plates creaked as opposing rocket-thrusts built up terrible strains, and on the vision screens the desert, spaceport, and alien vessel spun in wild confusion.

Deftly he steadied the plunging ship, and for a moment the tremendous helical construction showed clear and steady. It was enough!

From the turret the triple guns snarled their defiance, and the lancing beams of energy smashed directly against the glowing spiral. Again the heavy-duty weapons spat their triple shafts of destruction. Again! Beneath the ship green fire blossomed from the desert. It spread, engulfing the sombre black buildings, flowing out to the very desert itself in a tremendous wave of brilliant emerald flame.

High into the air the green energy roared. The turmoil of its passing flung the heavy ship aside and for a moment Caleb fought to prevent what seemed like certam destrucion. Then the flame died, the air quietened, and he gazed in wonderment at the vision screens.

The spaceport was gone!

All the humped black buildings, all the maze of eye-twisting structures, all had gone. A great pool of molten slag glimmered with evil emerald light in the midst of a circle of fused sand. A pool of slag that even as he watched began to solidify and crack. The sudden re-lease of energy from what must have been tremendous accumulators and storage banks, had wrought total destruction.

A fleck of green flame spun towards him. Automatically he threw the ship to one side, and then blasted frantically with all jets as the hull shuddered to the detonation of more alien weapons. In the vision scresns two vessels, their odd shapes covered with writhing lines of twisting green energy, darted towards him.

"Jenner!" Caleb spun in his chair and yelled to the big engineer. "Jenner, can you hear me?"

"What is it?"

"The intercom isn't working. How long before we can enter hy-perspace?"

"A few minutes, but Caleb, is it wise so near a planet?"

"No," admitted the captain. "But there are two ships after us, and I want to get away." He looked worriedly at the vision screen.

"I'm trying to run from them, but they can make as much speed as I can. I hope that they can't enter hyperspace now that their helix has been destroyed, but I could be wrong."

"I'll start feeding power into the coils now," promised Jenner.

From the turret came a snarling roar as Wilner fired the guns. The brilliant streak of energy barely touched one of the menacing vessels, but it spun away, the green lines of energy dimming on its hull. A second blast, and then the guns fell silent.

Within the ship tension began to build. Caleb watched as the alien ship drew nearer. From the truncated cones spat a shower of tiny green specks. They spun rapidly across the void, and despairingly Caleb knew that he couldn't avoid all of them.

His head ached and his eyes seemed to blur. Something grippwd his stomach, and the ship seemed to twist and move in odd dimen-sions. A faint whisper of sound began to echo from the deckplates and bulkheads.

They were in hyperspace!

Again came the mounting sensation of tremendous strain. The faint whisper grew louder, and the throb of power from the over-loaded hyper-drive shook the very structure of the ship Nausea gripped him, nausea and a terrible sensation pf being turned inside out. With abrupt suddenness the feeling passed.

Stars gleamed before him. A myriad of glittering points of vari-coloured lights. A yellow sun glowed from one corner of the screen and a green-tinted planet spun on its lazy orbit. Wilner came clattering from the turret.

"We're through!" He stared at the screen in wonder. "We are back in our own universe. 1 recognise that sun—I'd know it anywhere. It's Sol! And look! That green planet, that's the home planet. That is Earth!" A footstep behind him made Caleb turn. A girl smiled a him, a young girl whom he had last seen cradled in his arms. Armitage, who seemed strangely young, grinned over her shoulder.

Somehow, Caleb knew that he wouldn't regret the loss of the treasure.